The Tidal Road Mystery

The Tidal Road Mystery

Anthony Hontoir

DOWNWOOD BOOKS

Downwood Books
Downwood House, Marlpit Lane
Porthcawl, CF36 5EG

First published in Great Britain by
Downwood Books 2016

002

ISBN 978-0-9558041-1-3

Set in 11pt. Garamond

Printed and bound in Great Britain by
Clays Ltd, St Ives plc

Cover design by Steven Novak

CONTENTS

1   I Am Introduced To New Surroundings

2   I Sample Strong Ale

3   I Take A Walk Down The Lane

4   I Attend A House-Party

5   I Go Out In A Boat

6   I Hear Of A Tragedy

7   I Consider My Position

8   I Call On A Neighbour

9   The Investigation Begins

10   The Investigation Continues

11   I Receive A Visitor

12   The Investigation Moves To West Winds

13   A Conversation At The Skipper's Inn

14   The Investigation Goes To Saltcombe

15   I Receive Another Visitor

16   I Taste Belle's Cooking

17   Where is Charles Seabourne?

18   The Gunshot Resounds

19 I Go Aboard The *Sarah Jane* Again

20 I Witness A Disappearance

21 I Learn Of Jeremy's Return

22 Back To Saltcombe

23 I Discover How It Was Done

24 In Conclusion

1

I Am Introduced To New Surroundings

"Hello there!" called out a friendly voice, and I turned to see a young woman on horseback smiling at me from where she had stopped to let her chestnut mare have a drink in the river. "I haven't noticed you around here before."

I walked slowly across the tidal road to the river's edge and paused beside the lapping water. The tide was going out, and the road was gradually drying and would soon be completely passable until the tide came in again.

"I've only just moved to Watersford," I replied, and she allowed her horse to come nearer, its feet splashing in the shallow depths. "This is the first time I've had a chance to look around."

"I thought you must be new here," she said, looking down at me with an intent expression on her face. "Welcome to our little village. I'm Rachel Summers."

"How d'you do, Rachel, my name is Godfrey Sanderson," I said, returning the introduction. There was still a gap of several yards between us. "Sorry I can't shake hands with you."

She laughed and made a move to reach her right hand out, knowing that she was too far away. "Another time," she suggested. "If I come any closer, you'll get wet."

"This looks very unusual," I remarked, pointing towards the road a short distance away where it was still partly submerged beneath the ebbing river.

"It's not called Watersford for nothing," said Rachel Summers, relaxing her grip on the reins so that her horse could resume having a drink in the cool clear river. "Twice a day every day the tide comes in and covers the road. Then, twice a day every day when it goes out, the road dries for a few hours and people can drive up and down it again. Didn't anyone tell you that before you came here?"

"I'm afraid not," I answered with a rueful grin. "I've never seen anything quite like it before."

She sat high in her saddle, looking down at me, and I found myself studying her more closely. She was a very good-looking young woman aged somewhere in her mid-twenties, I estimated, and below her riding helmet she had long fair hair which blew gently in the light breeze. She wore a pair of old jeans which seemed to be rather strained at the thighs and were tucked into a pair of mud-splashed boots. I took an immediate liking to her, and could see that she was just as carefully studying me with an appraising pair of eyes that were impishly humorous.

"If you're wondering where it goes to," she said, "there's a little village called Smallbury a couple of miles further down the estuary, nearer the coast. Beyond that, of course, is Saltcombe. When the tide's in, it's a ten-mile detour, so most local people make sure they know the time of high water and plan their journeys accordingly. But when you have a horse," she added, "it doesn't really matter!"

"So it would seem," I replied with a laugh.

"Where are you living, anyway?" she asked. "I'm very curious to know what place you've got."

"I moved into Hill Cottage yesterday evening," I answered, indicating towards a narrow lane that joined the tidal road not far from the place where we were talking. This was my first exploratory walk since I had arrived with my few belongings, and explained how I was unaware of the existence of the tidal road until now.

"Very nice," she said approvingly. "It used to be old Mrs Harrington's place, but she died about six months ago. Her family spent a lot of money doing the place up. You're very lucky to have it, you know – quite a few locals wanted to buy it."

"I offered to do so myself, but it seems that the family preferred to keep the ownership of it. Apparently they had it in mind to turn it into a holiday cottage."

"You *are* in glorious Devon," said Rachel. "What do you expect?"

"Well, as I was thinking of coming to live here permanently, I was actually expecting to buy somewhere, but this will do for the time being. Do you live near here?"

"Not far away. My family's got a farm – in that direction." She pointed back along the way she had come, further down the estuary towards the sea. "We're just out for our early morning walk."

"It's certainly a beautiful day," I remarked, gazing around at the sunlit fields that covered the gently undulating hillside on the opposite side of the river, separated from each other by green hedgerows and small clusters of woodland.

"Are you married?" she asked suddenly. The question took me momentarily by surprise, but I saw no reason to reply with anything other than the truth.

"Not any longer," I said, and a quizzical look came over her. If I tell you that I have a daughter who was probably older than Rachel Summers, you will understand something of the difference in our ages, but as I had decided to make a new start in life, a fresh beginning as it were, I simply saw her as an attractive young woman. It would seem far less likely for someone in her position to show any interest in me, but vanity is a wonderful thing when it comes to convincing yourself of the seemingly impossible. I had taken early retirement, and prided myself in the fact that I did not look my age. It was only natural to reply likewise. "Are you?"

"Nobody will have me," she answered. I raised my eyebrows in an expression that was intended to show disbelief, and she gave a laugh. "Well, perhaps it's the other way around, really." She cast me a curiously thoughtful glance and grasped the reins. "I must be on my way now. I shall see you again soon, no doubt, Godfrey. Just for you to know, I work at The Skipper's Inn most evenings. Come and have a drink sometime."

"I look forward to it," I said, entering into the playful spirit of the parting. "Goodbye, Rachel. See you soon."

She turned and rode off along the receding river's edge and I watched her go, pleased that I had struck up an acquaintance so soon after my arrival in Watersford. She swayed effortlessly in the saddle to the rhythm of her horse's meandering walk, and quickly looked back over her shoulder to see if I was still watching her. "Don't forget!" she called, and gave a final wave of her hand.

I resumed my own wandering stroll along the tidal road, pondering on the fact that barely five minutes ago I had been a complete stranger to the district and now I had made a friend of someone in the most casual of circumstances. This business of moving to a new part of the country might turn out to be successful after all, I thought to myself, for I had certainly embarked on it with a degree of apprehension. Most of my possessions, the things that one accumulates during a lifetime, were in storage in the town of Beaconsfield, where I had lived quite happily for many years, although those days suddenly seemed far away and I knew that there would be no going back.

The river water was ebbing rapidly, leaving damp sections of the road covered in green slimy weed smelling strongly of the sea, and in places where the road ran higher, it was completely dry. On one side of the road were the emerging mud flats, and on the other side the ground rose steeply, with massive oaks and sycamores growing on the slope, creating a vast overhanging canopy of foliage. I considered that this picturesque scene of rural tranquillity must have appeared the same to generations of local people. The only feature that could in any way be described as modern was the presence of small yachts and sailing boats moored along the length of the river, some of which were now becoming stranded on sandbanks as the tide retreated, and even a few of these appeared to be quite old, including a wooden-built cabin cruiser that looked as if it had been made soon after the Second World War. In a few hours from now, when the next tide came in, they would be fully afloat once again. Meanwhile, cars and tradesmen's vans were beginning to appear on the road, making their way in one direction or another to and from Watersford, and there were convenient passing places every so often, otherwise for most of its length the road was only wide enough to allow for the passage of one vehicle at a time. I wondered how many drivers had misjudged the width of the road when it was partly flooded, and ended up in the mud. Probably quite a few, especially at pub closing time. The green riverweed added to the likelihood of a mishap, and I picked my way carefully over it so that I did not slide on the slippery strands and fall over.

I continued walking along the tidal road, following its haphazard route in fascination until it arrived at a place where it turned inland and began to go uphill. The small tributary of another river crossed it at this point, and mudflats stretched away on either side of the roadway, making it necessary to mark its position with a series of upright wooden posts, each set firmly into the ground, one opposite another, so that the road would be clearly marked out even at high water, when the tarmac surface was completely submerged. You could tell exactly how far the water rose above the level of the road by observing the familiar green weed growing on the lower part of each post, though I am aware that high and low water constantly changes in accordance with the moon, so that spring tides are higher than neap tides, each occurring twice a month. Evidently this was the most dangerous stretch of the tidal road, which could be inundated to waist height, far higher than would permit for the safe passage of any motor vehicle. Having never seen anything like it before in my life, I was intrigued to think that people living in this part of the world had to contend with it all the time. The presence of so many small boats moored along the river suggested that sailing was a popular pastime and perhaps, in some instances, a necessity.

As the road now began its ascent of the hillside I slowed my pace, thinking that it was time to turn around and make my way back to Watersford, but then I noticed a large house standing halfway up the hill, surrounded by trees, and it drew my attention. It was a magnificent building, designed in the style of Lutyens, and commanded a spectacular view across the estuary. I considered how lucky some people were to live in such a wonderful setting, and decided that the owner must be very rich to be able to afford a house like it. No doubt there were other mansions dotted about the surrounding countryside, each with its own secluded position, each providing its fortunate owner with a luxurious foretaste of heaven. Oh well, I had my comfortable rented cottage to go back to! I kept walking until I reached the grand gateway leading to the big house and saw that its name was set into the stonework of the pillars: it was called West Winds. I stood gazing at it through the trees for a few moments, glimpsing red brickwork, white-painted windows, tall chimneys and a tiled roof with a pleasing array of dormers. The entire scene had a picture postcard look to it and reminded me of something from the past – the days of wealth, opulence and extravagant house-parties in the hedonistic thirties. It was almost possible to imagine voices from long ago on the front lawn talking excitedly about the latest dance craze or stock market prices whilst storm clouds gathered over Europe. I smiled to myself, shook my head at the thought and turned to walk back to my little cottage at the end of a narrow lane in Watersford village. I had set out on a new life for myself in this quiet and beautiful corner of England, and wondered what the days ahead would bring.

2

I Sample Strong Ale

"Godfrey, you made it!"

"I could hardly ignore such a charmingly-delivered invitation," I said with a smile, "and on horseback, no less!"

Rachel Summers responded with a laugh. The Skipper's Inn was a small quaint pub with a low ceiling, and she was standing behind the bar, looking quite different from the way I had last seen her. In place of her riding outfit, she wore a black top with a low neckline and her blonde hair was tied back. A large pair of ear-rings and make-up completed the transformation.

"What can I get you to drink?" she asked, ignoring the raised voices of several locals trying to attract her attention across the bar.

"What do you recommend?" I inquired, looking at the row of illuminated beer taps.

"There's a very nice local ale," she said, pointing to one of the less well-known names. "I'd have that one, if I were you."

I nodded, and she began to fill a pint glass. The raised voices got louder.

"That's enough from you, Jack, and you, Tom," she called out. "Can't you see I'm serving this gentleman?" She turned to me and shook her head in mock despair before giving them a big smile. "Just wait your turn and I'll be with you in a minute!"

"Busy evening," I remarked.

"You should be here on a Friday or Saturday," said Rachel, placing the full glass down in front of me. "There's hardly any room to move in here then. We do very nice bar meals, too, if you ever feel tempted. The fish is all locally caught, and the vegetables come from around these parts too, when in season."

"From your own farm?" I asked.

"Of course," she replied with a laugh. "I can see you're catching on fast to our ways."

I took a sip of the dark brown ale and savoured the taste. "Hmmm, that's very good."

"Told you so," said Rachel before directing her attention quickly to one of the other customers standing at the far end of the counter. She made her way over to the man and I noticed that she was wearing a short black skirt that displayed a sturdy and yet attractive pair of legs. I allowed my gaze to wander up and down, admiring her from the blonde hair tied up at the back of her head with a big clasp to the painted toenails of her feet, visible in a pair of stylish high-heeled sandals. It was mid-evening and people were still coming into the bar. I had a few

18

polite smiles and muttered greetings from several men standing nearby and raised my glass in reply. Rachel called across to them: "Godfrey's new to the village – make him feel welcome!"

I joined the group and a conversation of sorts got under way, with a few questions asked, such as where had I come from, did I know the area at all and what had made me decide to settle there? Comments were thrown into the general conversational melee and I noticed that Rachel Summers kept returning to our end of the bar to make sure that I was not being left out and ignored. I got the impression that they were very friendly and when my glass was nearly empty they offered to buy me another, arguing among themselves as to who was going to do so.

Then the entrance door opened and four young people came into the pub, two men and two women, all in their twenties. I glanced up and noticed them waving to Rachel. She waved back, and they pushed their way through the crowd to get to the bar. There was a lot of excited chattering and laughing between them so they obviously all knew each other very well. After a few moments, Rachel beckoned to me and called across: "Godfrey, come and meet some friends of mine!"

I excused myself from the older group and stepped over to the bar where the four young newcomers had gathered. Rachel pointed to them in turn.

"This is Jeremy Seabourne, Emma, his fiancée, Catherine Seabourne, Jeremy's sister, and Robert Fairweather," she said, and they looked at me and smiled

19

politely. "Just for you all to know, this is Godfrey Sanderson, who's only recently come to live in Watersford."

I studied them all carefully, as I have a habit of doing with new acquaintances; Jeremy and Catherine, the brother and sister, though not exactly alike, had a certain family similarity in that they were both rather tall and broad, and had light brown hair, Jeremy's cut short, Catherine's tied back in a long ponytail. Emma was quite a bit smaller than Catherine, and had a trim, neat figure and friendly, smiling face that made you take to her immediately. Robert was a good-looking young man with a serious expression and demeanour but a humorous pair of eyes. He was starting to lose his hair, and this made him appear a little older than the others, although I assumed that they were all similar in age to Rachel, with Emma possibly being the youngest.

"Hope you like it here," said Jeremy Seabourne pleasantly, stretching out his hand to shake mine. His grip was firm and decisive, but the expression in his pale grey eyes seemed slightly condescending. The others quickly followed his example, and I returned their greetings with handshakes all around.

"I'm sure I will," I replied, adopting the same easy manner which seemed to be very much the local habit. "Does each of you live here in the village?"

"Some of us come and go," said Jeremy languidly, "and some of us stay here all the time." He looked at his three companions. "That's about right, isn't it?"

"What my brother really means by that," said Catherine Seabourne, looking at me with a slightly impatient air, "is that some of us actually work for a living and others don't. Jeremy does the coming and going whilst I work for a firm of solicitors in Kingsbridge."

"I used to work there, too," said Emma, joining in. "That's how we got to know each other, but I'm an estate agent now so I sell the properties and Catherine does the conveyancing."

I turned to Robert Fairweather. "And what do you do?"

"I work in Saltcombe," he replied. "What Catherine and Jeremy haven't told you is that their parents live in Watersford and they're filthy rich, which is why Jeremy chooses not to work but Catherine, the sensible girl that she is, thinks she ought to, on the off-chance that mummy and daddy's money might run out one day."

"Don't believe a word of it," said Jeremy in good humour. "Actually I work in London, but I spend quite a lot of my time here because I happen to like it in this part of the world. One can get so bored with London after a while."

I said I was inclined to agree with him, because I had spent a lot of my working life in the capital, and now all I wanted to do was to enjoy the quiet life. "Mind you," I added, "no sooner did I arrive here yesterday than I met up with Rachel this morning when she was out riding her horse, and I already feel that I'm part of village life." I turned to give Rachel a smile, and she beamed radiantly

21

back at me.

"Actually my parents are holding a house-party this weekend," said Jeremy, "which explains why I'm down. Most of the usual crowd will be there. Are you coming, too, Rachel?" I'm not sure whether I imagined it, but I thought I detected a trace of mischievous teasing in his voice. Emma, his fiancée, seemed not to notice anything. The next moment he turned to me. "You're welcome to join us if you feel like it. Might as well meet my old folk and see what you think of them. They love making new acquaintances of their own age."

"Thank you very much, I'd like to do that," I said. "Where do they live?"

"Not far from here, along the tidal road. First house on the right as you go up the hill."

I opened my eyes wider at the realisation that Jeremy Seabourne was referring to West Winds, the house I had admired through the trees. Rachel quickly interjected: "Godfrey can come with me if he likes."

I smiled at her across the bar. "Thank you," I said, and she gave me a certain look which made me wonder if there had once been something between her and Jeremy. I could best describe it as a look of triumph, as though she had achieved what she wanted in order to annoy him, but it might have been my imagination again. There was little doubt in my mind that he had tried to align me with his parents' generation in order to make a point, and yet I suppose this was a perfectly logical thing to do. After all, I *was* undoubtedly of their age and there was nothing to

22

be gained by pretending otherwise. A few moments later Rachel moved to another part of the bar to serve waiting customers. I carried on drinking my second glass of ale and began to feel the effect of its strength. It was most palatable, and I enjoyed the way it made for a more convivial atmosphere.

"That's all arranged, then," said Catherine Seabourne, giving me a smile and a nod of the head. "We'll look forward to seeing you on Saturday evening. It won't be a dress-up affair, you can come however you want to."

"I'm sure I have something suitable in the cottage," I said.

"If you don't mind my asking, whatever made you think of coming to a place like Watersford?" she inquired. "It seems to me that it's the sort of place you grow up in and that's that. I'd never come here myself if I didn't already live here."

"My family used to come to Devon for their holidays when I was young," I explained, "and I have always liked it in this part of the world. I used to tell myself that I would return and live here one day if I ever had the chance. Not necessarily to Watersford, but to the county. It so happens that my wife had no interest, but we separated recently after many years of married life. She decided she wanted to go her way so I've gone mine. Our daughter is married with a family of her own, and therefore I no longer have any ties or responsibilities. I feel as though I'm single and free again."

Catherine stared at me in wonder. "How fascinating,"

she said. "So you just happened to pick Watersford by chance? It could have been anywhere?"

"Within reason, yes," I replied. "Before I came down here, I made a lot of inquiries to try and find a nice little place to buy, but then I found Hill Cottage and settled for that, although it's only rented."

"I hope you like it here."

"Thanks. It's the idea of living near a river that appeals most of all, and I'd love to buy a little boat one day and sail it up and down."

"Sounds most romantic," laughed Catherine. "Actually my parents own one of the boats on the river, a cabin cruiser. They've had it for years, but they don't really bother with it much now. Jeremy takes it out occasionally, though, don't you, Jeremy?"

Jeremy turned to her at the sound of his name being mentioned, but he did not seem to have heard what his sister was saying. "What was that?" he asked, leaning forward.

"I said you still take the *Sarah Jane* out from time to time."

"Oh yes, whenever I feel like it. A trip down to Saltcombe and back, nothing more."

I caught a glimpse of Catherine glancing over to the bar, but Rachel was still serving drinks at the far end, and then her eyes flicked back to Emma who was standing beside Jeremy listening to the conversation but not saying anything.

"Are you keen on the water?" I asked her, and Emma

shook her head.

"Jeremy drags me out there sometimes, but I don't think it's much fun," she answered, and took a sip of her drink. "Besides, it's got something wrong with it these days. The engine doesn't work properly, or it leaks, I'm not sure which. It's made of wood, so it must be very old."

"Wooden boats are the best," said Robert Fairweather, joining in suddenly with enthusiasm. "There's craftsmanship in them that you don't see nowadays."

"You sound quite an expert," I said jokingly, "for someone so young."

"I work at Wallace's Boatyard in Saltcombe, so I know a lot about boat-building. Of course, everything's reinforced plastic these days, but I happen to prefer boats that were designed and built in a classic style – they look good. Actually, there are some boat-builders who still use wood even today, and we occasionally get one in for repair. If I could afford it, I'd have a wooden one myself. You can keep all these moulded hulls!"

"Robert gets some wonderful ideas in his head, but he'll never have one," said Jeremy.

"I might!"

"And what he doesn't tell you is that he's also a crew member of the Saltcombe lifeboat, and they gave up wooden boats years ago!"

The topic of conversation moved away from boats, wooden or otherwise, and I listened to them arguing about a few other matters before the evening was over.

They were obviously friends who enjoyed having different opinions. I cannot remember whether I was on my third or fourth glass of strong ale when time was finally called, but I know I was feeling pleasantly light-headed.

"Do you know how to make your way home from here?" asked Rachel, looking at me rather anxiously. "We don't want you falling in the river on your second day."

"I'm sure I can find my way back all right," I assured her, but she seemed doubtful.

"I'll drop you off in my car," she said. "It's parked outside. Just wait a few minutes for me to finish work. I shouldn't have suggested you having that ale, it's rather strong!"

I sat on a stool by the bar whilst everyone said good night to each other and drifted out. Rachel's four friends bade me farewell and assured me that they looked forward to seeing me on the weekend, and soon Rachel had finished her shift and told the landlord she was going home.

"Ready?" she asked, coming up to me and taking hold of my hand with a determined but gentle grip, and we went outside to where she had parked her little car in a corner of the pub's car park.

"They seem a lively crowd, those friends of yours," I remarked, settling in beside her.

"Oh yes, most of us have known each other for years," she said. "You don't always want to pay too much attention to what Jeremy says, mind, because he can be a bit strange sometimes, especially when he meets someone for the first time. He's rather shy, really, in spite of what you might think."

"Is that what you call it?" I said in a light-hearted voice. Rachel smiled and started the engine. It was half-past eleven and the tide was at its highest point, but in the darkness I could not make out anything beyond the beam of the headlights. Rachel drove up the narrow lane and soon we arrived outside the front door of Hill Cottage.

"Here you are, Godfrey, safely home."

"Thanks. Would you like to come in for a coffee?"

"That's very sweet of you, but I won't stay any longer – I've got to go and see to my horse last thing." She smiled at me. "Yes, I know it seems mad, but it's part of the routine before I go to bed. Our farm is only at the top of the hill, you see, and the fields overlook the river. You must come up and I'll show you sometime. My horse grazes in a field next to the stables, and has the best view of any horse for miles around." She sighed. "Anyway, I'd better go and make sure she's safely in her stable for the night."

"Good night, Rachel," I replied, opening the door of the car. "Thanks again for all you've done to make me feel at home here. It already seems as if I've been in Watersford for ages!"

"Good night, Godfrey," said Rachel, and she leaned quickly across the car to give me a kiss. "See you soon!"

And then she was on her way, the lights of her car disappearing up the lane, and I let myself in through the

27

front door, my mind preoccupied with the thought of exciting possibilities.

3

I Take A Walk Down The Lane

It was just after nine o'clock the following morning, while I was finishing a late breakfast at the kitchen table in my small cottage, that I heard a curious sound. It seemed to be a faint tapping and scraping, followed a few seconds later by the tinkling of a bell. I knew that there was a small brass bell hanging in the porch by the front door so I assumed that I had a visitor, and got up from the table to go and open the door.

Standing outside, a matter of inches from my face, was the inquiring head of a large horse, nose sniffing and ears twitching, and sitting high up in the saddle, holding her riding crop in one hand, was Rachel Summers. She had obviously tried knocking on the door with it but failed to make anything more than the indistinct noise I had heard, and decided to shake the bell instead.

"Good morning!" she greeted me with a friendly smile. "I hope I'm not too early. Gin and I are taking our morning walk down the lane into the village, and as we were passing by I thought you might like to come for a walk with us. It's a lovely morning and we can show you some of the local sights."

"That's a wonderful idea," I said. "Just give me a few moments to get ready and I'll be with you."

I hastily went back inside the cottage, put my breakfast dishes in the kitchen sink, picked up my jacket and joined Rachel outside in the lane.

"Nobody locks their doors around here," she said, "so don't worry if you haven't got your keys."

We set off along the lane, Rachel slowly riding her horse whilst I walked beside them.

"Did you enjoy your visit to our little pub last night?" she asked casually.

I nodded. "Yes, I thought it had a very nice atmosphere. The locals seem most friendly and welcoming."

"It's that sort of place, really. The pace of life is slow and everybody gets on with everybody else." She pointed ahead to a place where the lane went off in two different directions. "Let's go this way. It takes us into the village without having to go along the tidal road. You wouldn't be able to get through at the moment because the tide is in. I'd be all right, though," she added with a little laugh.

"Why is your horse called Gin?" I inquired after we had walked for a few minutes.

"It's short for Ginger. In fact she's chestnut, but you can see the tinge of ginger mixed in so that's what I decided to call her. It's got nothing to do with gin and tonic, although I think she's far better than any tonic I can imagine." Rachel reached forward and patted the long mane. "Aren't you, my lovely gorgeous thing?"

"Is she a well-behaved horse?" I asked, noticing that Gin didn't seem to mind my presence.

"She's a beauty," said Rachel, smiling happily. "Mind you, don't be fooled by what you see of her now – she's a typical red-head, so she can be flighty and fiery! But she's on her best behaviour this morning. She must like you already, Godfrey!"

We walked on in silence for a while.

"Have you always had a horse?" I asked suddenly, thinking that a farmer's daughter would be likely to.

"Oh yes, I grew up with them," said Rachel. "Before Gin, I had Sebastian – he was an Appaloosa gelding."

"A what?"

Rachel laughed at my puzzled expression. "A spotty horse!" she explained. "Very striking in appearance with a personality to match." Gin's head turned slightly and Rachel reached forward to pat her gently. "But he wasn't a darling like you, was he, my sweetie? Do you know, Godfrey, I've got to be so careful what I say in front of her!"

We carried on down the lane and passed a small building on our left, partly hidden amongst the trees and shrubs, which resembled a run-down shack, but when I studied it more closely I noticed that it seemed to be inhabited. Wisps of smoke rose lazily from the chimney, there were curtains in the windows and the small patch of front garden had flowerbeds with a colourful array of plants growing. I paused in surprise.

"Yes," said Rachel, seeing the look of amazement on my face, "someone actually lives there. You'll probably meet him one day, being a neighbour of yours, not that he goes out very much. Bit of an odd character. Apparently he used to be a well-known journalist working for one of the big dailies in London, but I don't know whether that's true. He turned up here after living for a while in Totnes. Personally I think he's a bit of a weirdo, but you can make up your own mind when you meet him, if you ever do."

We continued on our walk. Eventually the lane levelled out and we passed a few other cottages clustered around a small brook and Rachel called out hello to several people she knew. Soon the road led us into the village, with its narrow main street which was comprised mostly of houses and cottages, some of which had shop windows. There was a Post Office, a small general store and a ladies' hairdresser. I asked Rachel to wait outside for a few moments and called into the grocer's for a newspaper. "I like to do the crossword puzzle," I explained.

"There used to be a lot more shops here at one time," she said. "There was a place selling antiques, a chemist, a wool shop – but most of them closed down because village life has been getting increasingly difficult for years, at least if you're trying to run a business. If you want anything now, you have to go to Kingsbridge for it."

"Isn't that where your friend Catherine Seabourne said

she worked?" I said.

"Yes, she works at a solicitor's office in Fore Street. That's the trouble these days, there's so little for people to do if they *want* to stay here. I'm lucky because I was brought up on a farm, but even in agriculture there are fewer jobs now. But tell me, what did you used to do before you retired?"

"Me? Oh, I worked in films."

"Films? How exciting!"

I gave a rueful chuckle. "Not nearly as exciting as you might think. I'm a retired cameraman. Mostly it was a lot of hard work and long hours – we'd usually start very early in the morning and go on late into the evening, and often I was away from home for weeks at a time, especially with foreign locations. But it paid well, and I got to see different parts of the world, although after a while I found that the travelling became very tedious. There's all the heavy gear that you have to carry around. Believe me, Rachel, all the glamour of films is what you see on the screen, not what goes on behind the scenes!"

Rachel gave a deep sigh and shifted her position in the saddle. "You've quite disappointed me, Godfrey." Suddenly she perked up. "Did you work with lots of famous people?"

I laughed. "That's a question I always get asked! The answer is yes, I've worked with a lot of well-known actors and actresses. Some of them are delightful, unassuming people and others are a pain in the neck – but I'm not going to mention any names! And a few temperamental

33

directors can remain nameless, too!"

"Oh, what a shame, I was hoping to learn the secrets of the business. Do you miss it very much?"

I considered the question. "Well yes, you can't spend years of your life doing something without missing it when you stop, but sometimes you have to be prepared to accept change. And I spent so much of my time away from home that my family life suffered. I took early retirement thinking that I could prevent the job from harming my marriage, but it didn't work out that way. For all the good it did, retiring early, I might just as well have carried on."

"And where would you be today?"

"In some far-flung part of the world peering through a camera lens, I daresay, and holding a light meter in one hand."

"But you wouldn't be *here*."

I glanced up at her and she was looking down at me meaningfully.

"No," I agreed with her, "I certainly wouldn't be here. Somebody else would be living in Hill Cottage instead of me. You would have met an entirely different individual on your daily equestrian perambulations."

"Well," said Rachel, "all I can say is I'm glad you did what you did!"

I smiled at her and patted her on the side of her leg, which was level with my shoulder. "So am I."

We walked on in silence, the only sound being the regular clip-clop of horse's hooves on the hard road surface. I was considering the implications of our blossoming friendship and I think she was, too. It was a relaxed silence because we were completely at ease in each other's company. By now we were approaching the end of the main street and further down the road, near the village pond, stood the church, a nicely-proportioned Norman building with a short squat tower. I cast a professional eye over it, because for some reason I seem to have spent a lot of my working life photographing churches.

"My family has lived in these parts for hundreds of years," said Rachel reflectively, "and now most of them are over there." She inclined her head towards the churchyard. "Baptised, married and buried."

"And so the world goes on," I murmured, "with us and without us."

"Godfrey, this is turning into a very morbid conversation!" We both laughed. Onwards we went and the road began to bend to the left, heading out of the village. Occasionally a car went by, but there was little traffic. Up ahead I spotted a turning and Rachel pointed to it. A small wooden sign had the name Skylark Farm written on it.

"That," she said, "is the way to our farm. It's a rough track that runs for nearly a mile back in the other direction – the house has a lovely view over the estuary. Don't forget that you and I have both been invited to the Seabournes' house-party tomorrow evening. It starts at half-past seven. I thought it would be better if we went together, so would you like to pick me up at quarter-past? I've seen your little sports car parked next to the cottage! It's cute!"

"You've got a wonderful way of putting things, Rachel," I said in amusement. "Of course I'd be delighted to call for you, and then you'll be able to introduce me properly to everyone there."

"A word of caution – the Seabournes are very wealthy people and they tend to view everyone else as if they are the same, which obviously they're not. You might have noticed yesterday evening in the pub that Jeremy can appear to be a little – what's the word...?"

"Spoilt?" I ventured tactfully.

"Yes, spoilt – that's exactly what he is. Everything he's ever wanted in life he's been given. Catherine is different. She's far more practical and down to earth. She has her job in Kingsbridge because she *wants* to work, not because she *has* to."

"I seem to recall young Mr Fairweather commenting something to that effect last night, as though the family's wealth shouldn't be taken for granted. I must admit I'd only met them for a few minutes and I felt I was witnessing the beginning of a family row."

"Well anyway, come along and enjoy yourself – they're excellent hosts and there's always plenty to eat and drink, and they only serve good stuff. They might even have one or two other people there, because they usually invite regular visitors to their gatherings."

"Such obligations often befall the well-off," I said, and

pretended to make a heavy sigh. "I've known quite a few film producers who feel the necessity to flaunt their riches."

Rachel started to snigger.

"It's called seeing how the other half lives," she said, "and I love it!"

We followed a circular route through Watersford which eventually brought us past The Skipper's Inn and beyond that, the river, which was now well-flooded with the morning tide. We stopped near the place where we had met yesterday, only on this occasion most of the road was under water and it was impossible for me to proceed any further on foot, whereas previously it had been on the point of drying out. Rachel indicated to a sign beside the road nearby and said to me: "This is where we must part company. The quickest way for me to get to the farm from here is to go along the tidal road and then up a track – Gin's used to going through the flood, we do it most days. The best way for you to get back to Hill Cottage is by walking up that footpath which comes out on the lane further up, just a couple of hundred yards from your place. I'm not in work for two days so you won't see me at the pub if you go down this evening. Don't forget – pick me up at quarter-past seven tomorrow."

With a quick digging-in movement of her heels and a sharp word of command, she set off on her way and I followed her directions back to the cottage, where I resumed my plans for the day which mainly consisted of sorting out my belongings and putting everything where I

wanted it after firstly clearing away the breakfast dishes.
I have always been domestically well-organised.

4

I Attend A House-Party

At almost exactly half-past seven the following evening I sat at the wheel of my little open-topped sports car, heading along the tidal road. Beside me sat Rachel, wearing a long flowing dark blue chiffon dress and matching high-heeled shoes, looking a picture of sophistication. She also wore a pair of sapphire ear-rings and had a gold necklace with a small gemstone around her slender neck and a fine gold bracelet on her right wrist. My own choice of clothes was limited to the items I had packed into two suitcases, but I felt respectably casual in light grey summer trousers, an open-necked shirt and corduroy jacket.

I had picked Rachel up from her home at the appointed time and we were now completing the short journey to West Winds. I noticed with some anxiety that the incoming tide was beginning to cover the road, but Rachel dispelled any worries that I might have had.

"It's all right for another half an hour at least," she said. "There'll be a bit of water here and there, but nothing much."

"What about later?" I asked.

"That's a different matter – it'll be completely flooded by midnight," she said. "Which means we shall have to go back by the long way, but that always happens with the Seabournes' parties. Unless we stay the night, of course," she added, her last words spoken with just a hint of suggestiveness.

I drove on through the small eddies of water flowing across the surface of the road and took greatest care on the final stretch, between the wooden posts, where the tributary river was now spreading across the mudflats and covering the road to a depth of several inches.

"There's a low exhaust on this car," I said to her with a feeling of trepidation.

"We're fine," she replied, peering over the side to look at the small waves we were creating through the flood. "The road is level along here so there won't be any nasty surprises!"

We got through without incident and began to ascend the hill. The gateway to West Winds came up on our right and I turned in, steering the car along the narrow driveway until it opened out into a big circle beside the house. There were already several cars parked neatly around the far rim of the circle and I joined on to the end of them. When viewed from close quarters, the house was even more impressive in appearance than it had been when seen from the road. There was a curiously rustic look to the red brickwork of the walls and the tiling of the roof that seemed to match perfectly with its setting, almost as if it were only natural that a house of this sort should be there, unlike other buildings which stand out awkwardly from their surroundings. Whoever had built this place at some unknown time in the past had got it right in every respect. Even the guttering and downpipes had a classy finish.

We arrived to the sound of voices and laughter coming from the direction of a pair of open French windows leading out onto a terrace, so I assumed that the party was already well under way.

"Let's go and join them," said Rachel, jumping out of the car. The cool evening breeze blew across the driveway and caught in the folds of her dress, making it billow outwards. She laughed and smoothed it down. There was a look of excitement and eager anticipation on her young face. "Come on!"

I climbed out of the driver's seat and cast a glance at the other cars parked nearby, which were all new and expensive, and included a gleaming white Bentley which I later learned belonged to Charles Seabourne. Next to it was a Porsche, then a Mercedes and a Jaguar, followed by a few lesser marques. Mine was not exactly old, but did not qualify for the description of luxurious. I smiled to myself, and then Rachel was leading me determinedly towards the front door. She rang the bell and the door was quickly opened by Catherine Seabourne, holding a glass of wine in one hand. The two girls embraced each other warmly in the hallway, taking care not to spill any wine on the polished parquet floor.

"I saw you coming up the drive," said Catherine, turning to look at me. "What a super little car you've got!"

"I longed for something I couldn't afford when I was younger, and now I've got it," I said, and she smiled politely as if I had made a joke without realising that it was the truth.

"Do come and meet everybody," she said, and led us across the hall to a room where the loudness of the voices seemed to suggest that the hosts and their guests had been partaking of their drinks for quite some time. We entered the room, probably the last guests to arrive, and I gazed around at the faces of two dozen or more people, standing in groups with several lots of conversation going on at once. I quickly picked out the tall figure of Jeremy Seabourne, standing at the opposite end of the room by the fireplace with his fiancée Emma beside him, and Robert Fairweather across the room near the French windows, talking to another man who, like everyone else present, was unknown to me.

Upon our entering the room, an older man looked over in our direction and Catherine beckoned to him. He detached himself from his little group and walked over to us with a benevolent expression on his face.

"Hello, Rachel, my dear," he said in a soft melodious voice and gave her a kiss on the cheek. Then he turned to me. "And you must be Rachel's friend," he went on pleasantly, studying me closely. "I'm Charles Seabourne,

Catherine's father. She said you'd be coming. I'm delighted to meet you."

I introduced myself and shook his hand. He was tall and strongly-built, with dark hair that had mostly turned grey, giving him a distinguished, rather patrician look, and his upright bearing was almost military in its correctness. There was a steely gleam of determination in his pale blue eyes, which continued to look at me in an appraising manner. This was clearly a man who had made a success of life, and an air of confidence lay behind the outward show of geniality and bonhomie. We were, I suppose, of a similar age, but he had achieved far greater things than I had done, and I found myself wondering what exactly they might be to provide him with such a magnificent place as West Winds.

"Well, please come in, get yourself a drink and meet everyone else," he invited, reminding me in a strange way of the middle-aged man who tries to play the part of a rather amiable and avuncular host – the archetypal bumbling buffoon, indeed – whilst hiding the shrewd and cynical character beneath the superficial appearance. "We don't stand on ceremony here, you know. This is a very informal party – just a few friends invited around. Delighted you could come, though. Must introduce you to my wife. Bless my soul, where's she gone?"

"Mum's probably in the kitchen," said Catherine.

"Oh yes, she's organising all the food with Rosanna," said Charles with a slightly contrived gaze of absent-mindedness, as a stage actor might overdo it for the benefit of a theatre audience. "Never mind! You can see her later. Do excuse me, won't you, I'd better get back to my other guests. Catherine, be an absolute poppet and get some glasses from over there for Rachel and Godfrey, will you." He waved towards a table, where rows of assorted glasses, tumblers and bottles were neatly arranged, and turned to walk away.

"Follow me," said Catherine obligingly, and led us over to the drinks table. "Of course, this is more Rachel's kind of work."

"I'm having a night off," said Rachel indignantly. "Nearly every evening of the week I'm pouring drinks for other people."

"Would you allow me?" I offered with a courteous gesture, and Rachel immediately started giggling.

"A vodka, lime and soda, please, Godfrey," she requested, "and you don't need to go too easy on the vodka."

I got to work with the bottles and picked up a silver measure. "Single or double?" Rachel opened her eyes wider and gave me a quizzical look. I poured out two measures and added a dash of lime before topping up with soda water. "Ice and lemon?" I asked, and she nodded. Soon she had a glass in her hand and started sipping from it.

"Gorgeous," she said. "You can mix a drink for me any time you like."

I smiled my appreciation of the compliment and poured myself a glass of beer. Robert Fairweather

44

wandered over.

"See you made it, then," he remarked in his laconic voice, sounding almost bored.

"Yes, I made it," I said.

"See you made it, too," mimicked Rachel, pulling a face at him.

"I always do," he said with a sudden grin, and wandered off.

At that moment trays of food arrived, carried by young girls who looked as though they had been hired to act as waitresses for the evening, and they set them down on another table which was covered with a spotless white tablecloth. There were salvers of sandwiches, sausage rolls, pasties, slices of quiche, smoked salmon, little pots of caviar, cold meats, dishes of potato salad, coleslaw, cheese dips, baskets of bread rolls and more.

Following behind came a tall strikingly good-looking woman with a figure that could have belonged to a fashion model, and she made her way casually over to the table and carefully arranged the salvers and dishes to her liking. She was wearing a slinky red dress and a pair of expensive red high-heeled shoes. She walked with a graceful stride on a strong, athletic pair of legs and had the bearing of a confident and dominating woman. Her fingers, wrists and neck were adorned with gold jewellery. This, I decided, could only be Mrs Seabourne, and when she turned around from the table I fleetingly caught her attention before she looked away again. I could see a distinct likeness between her and Jeremy, who was standing a few feet away from her, although there was not much similarity with Catherine.

The man to whom Robert Fairweather had been talking when we arrived was now standing on his own, looking out of the French windows at the view across the estuary, and Mrs Seabourne seemed to be watching him, for her attention appeared to be centred in his direction. Everyone else slowly began drifting over to the cold buffet, but as Rachel and I had only recently arrived, I thought it would seem a little impolite to rush straight over and start eating immediately. Instead, we moved closer to the windows, where there was a pleasingly cool draught of air, as if to admire the view, and the man glanced at me.

"Beautiful evening," he said. "I don't think we've met before. The name's George Bland." Again there was a cordial shaking of hands. He merely smiled and nodded at Rachel, so they obviously knew one another. "There aren't many places with a view like this. I always tell Charles and Minkie how lucky they are. Do you sail, Mr – er, sorry, I didn't catch your name..."

"Sanderson, Godfrey Sanderson. No, I don't sail, but I've just come recently to live in Watersford, and I was telling Rachel and her friends only the other day that I'd love to have a boat of my own one day."

George Bland was a compact little man, perhaps fifty years of age, with a quiet self-assurance to his stance, and he was dressed in smart casual clothes that all looked well-made and expensive. He was wearing an open-necked blue striped shirt with a plain collar, a dark blue blazer and light grey trousers; his small feet were clad in a pair of hand-made black leather casuals. He had his limpid grey eyes on the small boats that were moored along the river towards Watersford in the distance. "Perhaps you will, Mr Sanderson, perhaps you will. I very much hope you do. It's a wonderfully relaxing pastime for those who enjoy that sort of thing. For myself, I much prefer to stay on dry land." He gently patted his stomach and made a facial expression indicative of seasickness. "Charles has his own boat, of course. It's on the river below the house." He pointed. "Down there, through the trees, but you can't see it from here. The *Sarah Jane,* it's called. I do like that name, it has such a friendly sound to it, don't you think?"

It was the small wooden-hulled cabin cruiser that Robert Fairweather had been talking about in the pub.

"If only I could see it, I'm sure it's a very nice boat," I commented conversationally.

George Bland turned to me with a flicker of a smile.

"Everything that Charles and Minkie own is very *nice,* as you put it."

"Have you known them long?"

"Oh yes, we're old friends from a long way back. Charles and I have done business together for years. I come down to stay here quite regularly. I'm sure you'll like Watersford very much, Mr Sanderson. I wish I could live here myself." He smiled again and prepared to move away. "If you'll excuse me, I think I must try some of their wonderful spread."

He turned and made his way towards the food table, seeming to glide silently over the floor in a movement that was reminiscent of a prowling cat.

I looked at Rachel and lowered my voice.

"Did I hear him aright? Did he say Minkie? Who's that?"

She nodded. "That's Mrs Seabourne's nickname, she's never known as anything other than that. Apparently she used to wear mink furs when she was young, before it became unfashionable to kill off lots of poor little minks, but the name has stuck."

"What am I supposed to call her? I can hardly say Minkie myself!"

"I don't see why not – everybody else does."

"Oh well, maybe it won't arise."

"I wouldn't be too sure," said Rachel, "she's coming this way."

I glanced up to see Mrs Seabourne heading in our direction with her purposeful stride. She certainly had an admirable figure for a woman of her age, and the cut of her dress displayed a bosom that many women half her age would have been proud to show off, or indeed paid good money to have artificially enhanced.

"Rachel! How lovely to see you! And this must be our newest arrival in the district," she said, giving me a sweet smile. "I'm so very pleased to meet you – I believe it's Godfrey, isn't it? My husband tells me he's already spoken to you. Now please do come and help yourselves to the buffet, don't be shy. Well, of course Rachel's like one of the family, really, aren't you, Rachel dear? Come along, Godfrey, this way."

Minkie Seabourne steered us both firmly across the room towards the table and put a plate in my hand with a folded linen napkin.

"Help yourself to as much as you like — that's what these house-parties are for, so that everyone enjoys themselves. Oh, and do drink up, there's plenty more beer or whatever you might fancy. Rachel, take care of Godfrey and make sure he has everything he wants. Now where did I put my own drink?" And the next moment Minkie Seabourne had moved off towards more of her guests, exhorting them to fill their plates and replenish their glasses.

"Better do as mother says," said a voice behind me, and Jeremy came up alongside with Emma closely at his elbow. "She'll be most put out if there's anything left over at the end."

I noticed he was not holding a plate himself.

"But aren't *you* having anything to eat?" I inquired.

"Guests first," he replied with a deferential bow. There was that slightly sardonic expression on his face again, and he looked across at Rachel. "Would you call yourself a guest, Rachel? I suppose you would nowadays."

Once again I sensed something in the atmosphere, but nobody else seemed to notice. Emma was looking lovingly at Jeremy with her usual show of adoration. I put my glass down on the table and started filling my plate, tasting one or two morsels as I went.

"The smoked salmon is delicious," said Emma helpfully, so I tried some.

"It is indeed," I agreed with her, and added some to the growing pile of food on my plate. She gave me her sweetest smile yet, like a child who has pleased a parent. A strangely innocent young woman, I thought, and not at all the sort I would have associated with Jeremy, but there you are – people often pair up in odd ways. Was I not doing the same thing myself?

The fine warm evening had tempted most of the guests to go out on the terrace, so Rachel and I decided to do likewise. I leaned forward to speak quietly in her ear.

"How do they come to be so rich?" I asked.

"Are you envious?" she answered mischievously.

"Not at all. Simply curious."

"Charles is a financier. Apparently he's made and lost several fortunes in his life. He's got friends in high places."

"They usually have."

"It's no good being jealous, Godfrey."

"I'm not."

Rachel shot me a quick look.

"Most people in Watersford are, and make no attempt to pretend otherwise."

"Are *you* jealous of their wealth?"

"Me? Why should I be? Does it make them happier? Does it make them better people?"

By now we were out on the front lawn, keeping

ourselves sufficiently away from everyone else to avoid being overheard.

"I've seen great affluence in others, and it often leads to arrogance," I commented.

"The Seabournes aren't really like that. Oh, they might like to show off a bit, but so do lots of other people."

"By having house-parties?" I suggested.

"Now Godfrey, that's naughty," said Rachel, giving me a disapproving glance. "You accept their invitation and then criticise them for it!"

"Actually the invitation came the other evening from their daughter," I reminded her, "and besides, I'm not criticising them. *You* said they liked to show off a bit, and I merely asked the question. Anyway, it's time to change the subject."

I had seen Catherine detach herself from talking to Jeremy and Emma and start coming towards us.

"Are you enjoying yourselves?" she asked, looking mostly at me.

I acknowledged the question with a gentle nod of the head and a charming smile. "Very much, thank you, Catherine. I was only saying to Rachel a moment ago what a wonderful evening this is." I felt Rachel give me a surreptitious dig in the side, and turned to her. "Wasn't I just saying that?"

"Oh, you were, Godfrey," said Rachel, pulling a face which I wasn't certain whether to take as a glare or a grin, but I think it was the latter.

Catherine took Rachel by the hand to pull her away.

51

"Would you excuse us for a minute?" she said to me. "I want to ask Rachel something."

She took her across the grass to Jeremy and Emma and they began talking. Standing further away, alone and looking at the view, was George Bland. For some reason he didn't seem to fit in, but perhaps I gave that same impression myself.

5

I Go Out In A Boat

"Somebody's suggested going out on the river before it gets dark!" said Rachel excitedly, returning to me. "Shall we go too?" She reminded me of my daughter when she was a child, full of enthusiasm to do something and not willing to have the idea dismissed. It made me smile to myself.

"Yes, if you like," I said, for I really didn't mind what happened. I was a complete stranger to the household and therefore not in a position to decide on the course of the evening's events, but I thought that a trip on the river sounded the perfect way of enjoying the party from a different perspective. Rachel knew that I had an interest in boats because I had already told her of the fact, so my assent came as no surprise. "When are they going?"

"Now, in a few minutes. They're just making up their minds about who's going. It should be fun!"

"But will it be safe?" I asked anxiously, remembering something that Emma had said in the pub.

"Safe? Well, yes, of course. Why shouldn't it be?"

I scratched my head reflectively.

"When we were all at The Skipper's Inn the night before last, the subject of the boat came up and I happened to ask Emma if she enjoyed going out in it. Apparently Jeremy takes it out whenever he feels like it, or at least he used to. Emma said there was something wrong with it, that's all."

"Oh," said Rachel in surprise. "I wasn't aware of that. What's supposed to be the matter with it?"

"She mentioned it leaking and the engine not working properly."

Rachel looked at me doubtfully.

"I don't imagine they'd suggest going out in it if it was about to sink or break down!" she said. "Emma must have been making it up – she gets strange ideas sometimes."

"In that case," I said, making up my own mind, "let's go. Besides, the river can't be *that* deep if we do sink!"

Rachel smiled.

"Exactly," she said.

A small group was gathering on the front lawn, and I could momentarily picture this sort of thing happening before in the past. I could almost hear those distant long-gone chattering voices again: "Let's go boating!" "I say, why don't we take a trip down to Saltcombe?" and "Make sure we put the jolly old hamper in and plenty of champagne!" Ghosts from a past era seemed to be in the midst of us, urging us on. Jeremy was holding forth, with Emma as usual by his side, looking adoringly up at him, showing no sign of concern about its safety now, and Catherine was there, too, with Robert Fairweather standing slightly apart. Two others came strolling up, a young married couple called James and Julie Carvell – a name that seemed quite appropriate in the circumstances. James was tall, slim, fair-haired and rather athletic in appearance, Julie was short, plump and dark, with a pleasing, one might almost say homely countenance, and she wore a pair of large, black-framed spectacles. Whereas James was dressed in a smart blazer and white summer trousers, Julie had chosen to go out in a somewhat shapeless red blouse, a dark frilly skirt and tight black leggings, as if she did not want to take too much trouble to make the best of herself.

When I heard Charles Seabourne, who had stepped out onto the terrace, declaring loudly: "Let all the young people go while we older folk stay here and open some more bottles," I wasn't sure if he was including me in one category or the other. George Bland stood by the French windows watching us impassively, and I wondered if he secretly wanted to come along with us, in spite of his allusion to a weak stomach in matters to do with sailing, but felt in any case that age ruled him out from taking part in the river trip. In a way it seemed as though I were amidst a children's party and they had just finished their tea and wanted to go and play with their favourite toys. Oh well, I thought, why not – you're only young once. It's how the privileged few behave in every generation, so why shouldn't I pretend to lose a few years and join the fun?

There was no organisation about it, we simply formed up in a small crowd and Jeremy set off as the leader, taking us down a steep narrow footpath which began at the edge of the front lawn and led us ever downwards, past tall trees and thick shrubs, until we reached a small gate at the bottom end of the boundary wall. We crossed the road and headed off again along another path which quickly brought us to the riverbank. The *Sarah Jane* was immediately visible, moored in the middle of the river and now fully afloat. A small wooden jetty had been built out from the muddy embankment and there was a tiny dinghy fastened to one of its upright wooden posts. The dinghy provided the only means of getting out to the cabin cruiser, short of wading through deep water, for it lay at its mooring some twenty yards from the bank.

Jeremy deftly detached the dinghy from the jetty and placed it in the water, still tethered to the woodwork by a length of rope. Then, in a well-practised movement, he lowered himself into the little craft, picked up two oars and cast off.

"I'll be about ten minutes," he called out, and paddled off in the direction of the *Sarah Jane*. When he reached it, he clambered on board and hauled the dinghy up on deck. For a couple of minutes he disappeared from view and then came back to the small cockpit. The evening silence was broken by the sound of the engine starting up and this was followed by the steady rhythmic burbling of the exhaust. He untied the mooring rope and a minute later the *Sarah Jane* was slowly approaching the jetty. He threw a line towards us and Robert caught it, pulling it taut until the side of the little cabin cruiser came close enough for us to get on board. The girls were giggling and squealing a good bit, trying to judge the best moment to step from solid ground on to the gently-rocking deck, and landed in the well of the boat with a lot of relieved laughter. I stood back for James Carvell to go ahead of me as he was still firmly holding his young wife's hand and Robert came last, jumping nimbly off the jetty onto the deck. No doubt he was used to encountering far worse conditions with the lifeboat and took it all in his stride.

"All aboard?" called Jeremy, glancing back over his shoulder.

"Aye aye, captain," replied Catherine, only too familiar with her brother's somewhat pompous manner, and Jeremy opened the throttle and turned the wheel.

Rachel took hold of my hand and gave it a squeeze.

"Where to?" asked Jeremy, raising his voice above the noise of the engine.

"Saltcombe, if there's time!" shouted back James, and everyone gave their agreement.

"Saltcombe it is, then," said Jeremy. "We've got plenty of time – high water isn't until quarter-past one."

We set off down the river, steering a course that kept us well clear of any other boats that were moored in the centre of the channel and not too close to the riverbank either, where the depth of the water was still uncertain because of the rising tide, although I imagine Jeremy knew where all the submerged sandbanks were. Our speed increased and the fresh evening breeze blew against my face, making me feel invigorated and filled with pleasure. I let go of Rachel's hand and put my arm around her waist, pulling her closer to me. The wind was blowing her hair everywhere, and she kept tossing her head back to stop it from going in her eyes. Catherine and Emma were laughing and doing the same; James was standing behind Julie with his arms over her shoulders, holding her tightly against him with his chin resting on top of her head. She snuggled up to him, arms folded so that they pressed his hands into her breasts.

Robert had gone below through the small cabin doorway without anyone noticing, and now he reappeared with a big grin on his face, holding up two bottles. It was an unexpected shock for me to see that they were, indeed, bottles of champagne, and rather expensive ones at that. A loud cheer went up and he popped the first cork, which flew with explosive gusto into the evening sky. Out came the glasses, too, and we all toasted ourselves.

"Here's to a damned good evening afloat!"

"Let's drink to a safe voyage!"

"Saltcombe and back!"

"To Julie." That was James's voice speaking, in a low voice.

"To James." That was Julie's reply. They were obviously still very much in love with each other.

"To us."

This last one was from Rachel, spoken quietly, and I looked down to see her staring steadily into my eyes. There was no doubting the meaning of it and my heart began to beat faster. I met her gaze with equal frankness and honesty, and touched my glass against hers.

"To us," I whispered in her ear, and then I noticed that Jeremy was watching us. He had turned away from the wheel for a moment and was looking directly at us. I felt immediately embarrassed and tried to pretend that I was unaware of having been seen.

"To *everyone*," he said slowly.

"What about me?" Emma's high voice spoke up, and her shrill protestation brought a burst of laughter from all on board.

Jeremy gave an exaggerated bow.

"To my dear Emma," he said, and there were more loud cheers. The boat gave a lurch and Jeremy quickly turned back to the wheel.

"Be careful!" shouted Robert, grabbing a handrail for support. His voice was sharp and possibly a little impatient and annoyed, for I suspected that his rather earnest attitude did not approve of levity whilst on the water. He was probably thinking of all his precious wooden-hulled boats, in the abstract sense of not being a boat-owner himself, but an admirer of the type. I reckon that theoreticians like him could be a lot less tolerant than the more practical seafaring men.

The *Sarah Jane* resumed her course down the river. The

reason for the sudden movement was that we must have caught a cross-current, for the river at this point had widened and begun to turn. Jeremy became more serious again, and I saw him refuse a re-fill of his glass when Catherine offered it, for she now had possession of the second champagne bottle. Drunk in charge of a boat on the river, I thought with some amusement, wouldn't look good in the local magistrates' court.

It took half an hour to reach Saltcombe, by which time the estuary had widened considerably and the surface of the water had become choppy as we approached the sea. The evening was getting darker by this time, and the lights of Saltcombe were twinkling on the side of the hill to starboard, making for a very pretty sight. Now that the sea was quite near, the breeze was picking up and becoming chilly. It was agreed that we had travelled far enough and should soon begin the journey back up the river. Jeremy started to make a slow lazy turn in the mouth of the estuary, taking care to steer well clear of the dozens of boats, large and small, which lay at their moorings. Saltcombe was a popular place for boating, being on a sheltered part of the coast within easy reach of Torbay and Plymouth.

We passed a few yachts with people on board, some under way, others tied up, and exchanged the friendly slow waving of outstretched arms; there were also distant calls of hello, mostly lost to the salt-laden sea air, and we replied with loud shouts of our own.

The homeward journey was faster, for we were

travelling now with the flow of the incoming tide, which seemed to exert a greater influence than the out-flowing of the river, and we had the wind behind us. The dusk sky still held just enough light to navigate safely and the course of the river was easy to discern, even in the gloaming, when the brightest objects to be seen were the beams of car headlamps on the road and occasional pinpoints of illumination from remote houses spread at irregular intervals across the landscape. In the growing darkness Rachel was hugging me tightly, though whether in affection or nervousness, or to keep warm, I was unable to tell. Perhaps a bit of everything.

Journey's end was marked by a return to the little wooden jetty, and in the closing moments of the trip Catherine gathered up the glasses and took them below with the empty champagne bottles. The procedure of disembarkation was almost an exact reversal of our boarding the boat earlier, Robert firstly alighting with the rope to pull us firmly against the landing, with myself getting off next to give him some assistance, James following, holding Julie's hand, and then the same excitable cries from the three girls, only more so this time for the darkness made it more hazardous and there was the added effect of the champagne. I held each of their hands to steady them. Once we were all safely ashore, Jeremy took the *Sarah Jane* back to her mooring in the middle of the river and I admired his clever use of the boathook and a handheld torch which quickly enabled him to secure the craft to the buoy. It was almost completely dark now, and a few more minutes passed before we heard the gentle splashing of oars and he came gliding out of the shadows in the tiny rubber dinghy. Robert helped him out of the water and together they fastened the dinghy back in its place.

"How did you enjoy your first trip on the river?" asked Jeremy, looking over at me.

"I enjoyed it very much, thank you," I answered. "It's a lovely river and I hope to spend a lot more of my time on it one day. You have a most attractive and well-behaved boat."

"It belongs to our father, of course," said Catherine. "He bought it years ago. It used to be on the Thames."

"Henley," added Jeremy. We began to walk back up towards the house. Small electric lights lit the path in the grounds of West Winds so that we could see where we were going. "He sailed it all the way down the Thames and then out into the English Channel when he bought it. The weather turned rough and our mother thought she wasn't going to see him again, but the old boy made it. Mind you, he was a good bit younger in those days. Catherine and I grew up listening to tales of that epic voyage."

"They used little boats just like the *Sarah Jane* at Dunkirk," said Robert, sounding singularly unimpressed. "They were built to withstand all kinds of conditions. Wood, of course. Can't beat it."

"From what I remember hearing about it," I said, "I seem to recall that a lot of those little boats were lost at

Dunkirk."

"Because they were fired on and sunk, not because they weren't well-built!" answered Robert.

"But it must already have been quite old when your father bought it," I said to Jeremy and Catherine.

"It was," said Jeremy. "And it needed a lot of repair doing to it. Some of the timbers in the hull were coming adrift and it was leaking quite badly. Wallace's Boatyard in Saltcombe, the place where Robert now works, took it in to fix it. Of course, that was years ago. They said it was a wonder it got here, and reckoned it should never have been sold in that condition. You can guess what our mother thought when she heard that! She still goes on at him about it."

"It looks as good as new now," I commented.

"Oh, it is. They repaired it very well."

"That proves my point," said Robert tiresomely. "Timber is the sovereign of boat-building materials. Ask anyone from the Vikings down, they'll all tell you the same thing. Even James knows – his name is Carvell!"

"Actually I think that's a coincidence," said James quickly. During the short pause in conversation, whilst we continued our ascent of the sloping footpath, I could imagine the look of puzzlement that probably crossed Julie's face, although she was walking ahead of me next to her husband.

"James, what does he mean?" she asked in a supposedly quiet voice, which still managed to make itself heard by all of us.

"Carvel with one "l" is a boat-building term, dear, I've told you before."

"Yes, but—"

"It's a method used for planking the hull," explained Robert. "I could go into more detail, if you like."

Rachel was walking beside me and I deliberately slowed my pace to let the others go on ahead.

"Oh dear," I said quietly to her, "I wish I'd never mentioned it now!"

"You've given Robert something to talk about for the rest of the evening and he'll bore everyone to death," she agreed. "It's very odd, though."

"What is?"

"Oh, just something I noticed earlier – it's probably my imagination. When Jeremy lost control because he was too busy staring at us, Robert almost fell over and grabbed hold of a rail to steady himself, but when I used to go out in the *Sarah Jane* with Jeremy, I don't remember the rail being there, I thought it was in a different position. Never mind. The important thing is, have you enjoyed yourself tonight?"

"Yes, very much. How about you?"

Rachel nodded and took a firmer hold on my arm.

"When we get back up to the house," she said, "I want you to mix me another vodka, lime and soda, just like the last one. But before that, I want you to kiss me."

We stopped on the footpath and the voices of the others receded in the distance. I turned to look at Rachel, and there was an intensity in her eyes that made my pulse quicken. She knew what she wanted and she was determined to get it. We stood among the trees clasped in an embrace. Her lips were warm, moist and inviting. Vaguely, in the back of my mind, I wondered what my ex-wife would think if she knew what I was doing now – even though it was all over with her. It was the first time in my life to do it out of doors and in somebody else's garden.

Once our desires were satisfied, we carried on strolling up to the house, across the front lawn and in through the French windows. The party was still in progress, the voices a little bit louder and jollier than earlier, and I went over to the drinks table to mix Rachel her vodka, lime and soda whilst she discreetly retired to the cloakroom. I expected to hear Robert Fairweather's voice still talking about boats, but there was no sign of him.

"He left soon after we came back," said Jeremy when I mentioned it. "Said he had an early start in the morning and didn't want to be late."

So we were to be spared the interminable details of boat construction and spent the rest of the evening in convivial conversation about everything and nothing. At half-past eleven Rachel and I made our excuses to leave – she said she would have to go and see to Gin last thing before bedtime – and we set off in my car on the ten-mile journey to cover a distance of less than a mile because the river was in full flood.

I dropped her back at the farm at ten minutes to midnight and she leaned across to kiss me goodnight. I remember hearing the softly-spoken words of endearment when she whispered "I love you" and I said "I love you too" back to her and then she was gone.

6

I Hear Of A Tragedy

The news that something awful had happened reached me the next morning when I walked into Watersford to buy a newspaper and bottle of milk in the village shop. I had already noticed a police car parked near the entrance to the tidal road and thought nothing of it. But word was quickly spreading around the village that a body had been found in the mud at the river's edge by the side of the road. A local man had found it at six o'clock when he was taking his dog for an early morning walk.

Somehow I knew it was Rachel. I cannot explain how I knew, but I was certain of it even before any details emerged. There were rumours of it being a young woman, although the man who discovered the body had not recognised it, probably because it was covered in thick slimy mud. But Rachel had been reported missing by her parents, and these facts were now in circulation. The tidal road had been closed to traffic and part of it cordoned off. It was possible to see a large police tent from the main road that ran over a river bridge several hundred yards away, where representatives of the press had gathered to set up cameras and take pictures, and several senior police officers were already in attendance.

The awfulness of it was made worse by the fact that I knew nobody there, apart from my few acquaintances at the party, and felt completely isolated with no one to talk to. What should I do? There seemed little point in doing anything other than returning to Hill Cottage, where I was sure that I would soon receive a visit.

The first police officer called in the middle of the morning. I opened the door to a young man in plain clothes. He seemed a bit uncertain of how to introduce the subject, as he had no clear idea about me other than having been informed that I knew Rachel Summers. But his presence at the door confirmed my worst fears.

"Good morning, sir," he began. "I'm Detective Sergeant Hoskins from Devon and Cornwall Police. I wonder if I might trouble you for a word, Mr...er...Sand...Sander..."

"Sanderson. Godfrey Sanderson."

"Oh yes, of course. I'm sorry, sir, I didn't quite know what your name was. May I come in?"

I stood back to let him in and we went into the living room.

"It's rather a difficult question I have to ask you, I'm afraid, Mr Sanderson, but are you acquainted with a certain Miss Rachel Summers?"

"Yes, I am," I replied, feeling myself becoming tense, my voice unsteady.

"Do you know her well?"

I couldn't think what to say straightaway, so it must have seemed that I blustered. "Er, not exactly *well*, but yes, I do know Rachel. We met a couple of days ago." My mind was spinning. What day was today? Sunday, of course. "I only moved to Watersford last Wednesday."

"I see, sir, so you're very new to the district?"

"Yes. I moved here from a place called Beaconsfield, not far from London."

Detective Sergeant Hoskins paused while he absorbed the information.

"I regret to say, sir, that a body has been discovered this morning in the locality, and it so happens that Miss Summers has been reported missing from her home. Naturally, sir, at this early stage we cannot give out any details until there has been a formal identification of the deceased, but I'm sure you understand that inquiries are being made into the circumstances of the death. And in case there is any connection between the finding of the body and Miss Summers's disappearance, we are trying to learn as much about her as possible. Would you be available at any time for further questioning, sir?"

His eyes were staring straight into mine with the unwavering gaze of a professional inquisitor, and those last words left little doubt in my mind that any investigation would lead directly to me. It was a nightmare that seemed to be worsening by the minute.

"Well yes, certainly, if you think I can be of any help," I replied.

"The thing is, Mr Sanderson, from what we have been told this morning during our preliminary inquiries, I gather that you and Miss Summers were seeing quite a lot of each other. Would that be a correct thing to say, sir?"

"Yes, I suppose it would," I said. "But really, Sergeant, I'm still finding it rather hard to take all this in. I was in the village earlier this morning to buy a couple of items in the shop and I heard that someone had been found dead. Please, can you tell me, is it Rachel or not?"

Hoskins's face did not give anything away at all.

"As I said just now, sir, we're not in a position yet to link the disappearance of Miss Summers with the finding of a body. Formal identification..."

"Yes, yes, I know all about that! Look, how can I put this? Rachel and I might only have met a few days ago – before that we were completely unknown to each other – but we had quickly become close friends. I'm sick with worry about her!"

"I understand how you feel, sir, but unfortunately I have to do things by the rules and those rules state that we should not jump to hasty conclusions, no matter how it may appear."

"You mean it might not be Rachel?" I asked with a faint vestige of hope.

"It was not my intention to imply that, Mr Sanderson. We have a way of carrying out our inquiries when things like this happen and in the early stages it is often difficult to confirm certain details, but inquiries still have to be made. If you don't mind my saying so, sir, you appear to be very concerned."

"I *am* very concerned! It might only have been a matter of a few days, but I felt that Rachel and I had something going between us!"

"I see, sir. In that case your impatience to know is perfectly understandable, but I would also like to point out that Miss Summers's parents and family are equally in a very upset state and anxious to have whatever news they can as soon as possible."

"I'm sure they are," I said quietly. "I'm sorry if you think I was being precipitate. I didn't mean to be selfish."

Hoskins's stolid manner was completely unmoved.

"You're not to be blamed for being worried, sir," he said, and produced a small notebook from his pocket. "Now then, sir, it would be particularly helpful if you could answer a few questions for me to be going on with. It will assist my superiors in deciding if there is anything else they need to ask you at a later stage. Would you mind very much, sir?"

In different circumstances I might have taken quite a liking to this bluff young man with his determinedly officious attitude. He was the sort, I felt, whose patience could be tried to the point of exhaustion, except that you'd never reach that point.

"Go ahead," I said, "ask whatever you wish."

"I need to find out a bit more about yourself first, sir. Your name is...Godfrey Sanderson..." He wrote it down slowly and carefully in his notebook. "I take it that the spelling is quite straightforward, Mr Sanderson?"

"Exactly as it sounds."

"And your address is Hill Cottage...Watersford. Would this be your permanent address, sir?"

"Well, I've only been here since last Wednesday, but it is intended to be, yes."

"And what would your occupation be, sir?"

"Retired. I used to work as a cameraman."

"Really, sir? I've not met any of those before. Interesting occupation, I would think?"

"Pardon? Oh, yes. Just like any other in the end." I found myself wondering if he was going to ask the usual question about working with anyone famous, but his face remained straight and serious. He wasn't the type to do so, at least not whilst on duty.

"How did you come to meet Miss Summers?" he asked, looking directly at me, his eyes scrutinising me carefully.

"It was quite by chance, actually. I arrived here fairly late on Wednesday and on Thursday morning I decided to begin the day by having a walk around to explore the surroundings. Rachel – that is to say, Miss Summers – was out riding her horse and she stopped for a chat. I told her I was new to the village and she did her best to make me feel welcome. She said she worked at the local pub and suggested I should call in for a drink. I suppose she thought it would be a good way of getting to know people. Well, I went there that same evening and several of her friends turned up. She introduced me to them and we got talking. The next thing I knew, I had been invited to a party at the Seabournes' house, which was yesterday evening. I arranged to pick up Rachel in my car and take her there. Afterwards, I dropped her back at her parents' farm. That was the last time I saw her. It was a few minutes before midnight."

The sergeant continued writing laboriously in his pocket notebook. He went on for some time while I sat watching him.

"There's nothing more I can tell you other than that," I said.

"Would you say you were in a relationship with Miss Summers, sir?" he asked suddenly, looking up at me, and my mind flashed back to the wooded path leading up to West Winds. A relationship? How was I to answer that?

"If you mean...did we have sex..." My voice trailed off and his eyes stared straight into mine without wavering. I nodded.

"I'm not trying to be offensive by asking these questions, sir, but you must understand that they have to be asked. It's the only way I can build up a picture of her last few hours, and there will be a very detailed forensic examination of the body." That seemed confirmation in itself – by his choice of words he had inadvertently indicated that it *was* Rachel's body lying out there. I clenched my fists tightly but said nothing. Oh, all right, if I wanted to put a different interpretation on it, I could try and convince myself that he was attempting to build up a picture of the last few hours of a missing person, but if Rachel had inexplicably vanished and a body had been discovered, who else was it likely to be? My mind, in a

73

state of shock, was going around in circles and thinking illogical thoughts. "There's one last thing I have to ask you, sir, and that is your age."

I told him, and I could judge from his momentary pause that he was working out in his mind the age difference between Rachel and myself. It was a gap big enough to make many people think dubious thoughts, and I daresay the sergeant's inquiries had already prompted a few comments. "Old enough to be her father," was the thought undoubtedly going through his head.

"Very good, sir, I think that's all for the time being. We will, of course, inform you of any developments as soon as they happen. In the meantime, I would be greatly obliged if you don't travel too far from here. Is there a telephone number we can ring to contact you? A house or mobile number?"

The telephone was standing on the window sill of the living room – I hadn't even had time to use it yet. I walked over to it and recited the number to the sergeant, and he dutifully copied it down. Then I took my mobile phone out of my pocket and gave him the number for that, too. He finished writing, snapped his notebook shut and slipped it back into his pocket.

"Oh, one last question before I go – I noticed a car parked next to the house when I arrived, Mr Sanderson," he said. "Would it be yours, by any chance?"

"Yes, it's my car."

"Do you mind if I have a quick look at it on my way

out?"

"By all means." I led the way around to the side of Hill Cottage where my little car was parked under a small lean-to covered area. I unlocked it and Hoskins opened the passenger door to peer inside, paying particular attention to the floor, then he went around to the back and looked in the boot. Finally he examined all of the tyres.

When he was satisfied that he had seen everything he wanted to, he turned abruptly and said to me: "It's quite possible the car will be needed for further examination and for that reason I must ask you for the keys. It must be kept locked and not touched. Do you have a spare set of keys too?"

"Yes, they're in the house."

"If you wouldn't mind, Mr Sanderson. I'll give you a receipt for them." He attended to the paperwork while I went to fetch them. When I returned, he handed me a slip of paper. "I'm very sorry, it's always a dreadful business when something like this happens. Expect to hear from us again soon."

And with that, Detective Sergeant Hoskins departed in order to carry on with his inquiries.

7

I Consider My Position

It was only a matter of time before the police established that the body found lying face down in the mud at the side of the tidal road was that of Rachel Summers. She was dressed in the same clothes that she had worn to the Seabournes' house-party, but her feet were bare. She was still wearing her ear-rings, necklace and bracelet. The cause of death was a single stab wound in the back from a sharp implement, although no weapon had been found. These were the details given to the press, and it appeared on the local television and radio news. Eventually it would be in the newspapers.

I was in a complete state of shock for some time, and could do little else other than pace up and down my living room floor, hour after hour, trying to grasp the reality of it, for it seemed bizarrely unreal and I kept trying to convince myself that at any minute I was going to awaken from a bad dream.

After a while, when my mind had cleared a little, I began to wonder what other people were saying. "Have you heard? The farmer's daughter from Watersford has been murdered!" "What? You don't mean the Summers girl? Do they know who did it?" "No, but the police think they've got a good idea. It seems that she became very friendly with some chap who's just come to live in the village. They even went to a party together, and some of the other guests are saying they were, well, you know, having a bit of a thing about each other – kissing and all that. Can't imagine what a young girl would see in an older man. Not one of *his* age." Gossip – nothing but gossip, and most of it harmful, even if some of it *were* true. All right, I'll admit it, I *did* fall for her, but what's wrong with that? It doesn't mean that I had any reason to murder her. If people knew that it was a genuine friendship blossoming quickly into a feeling of mutual love and affection, they would realise that I had no wish to harm her. Good heavens, it would be my only desire to protect her!

But how could I be anything other than the main suspect? It was already apparent that her father and mother had not seen her after the time she set off for the Seabournes' house-party with me, and there was no indication that her bed had been slept in that night, so one could only assume that she didn't arrive back home later. Her parents had gone to bed themselves at around half-past ten, so they wouldn't have heard me dropping her off just before midnight – as far as they were concerned, she went out and didn't come back.

Witnesses at the party would state that the last time she

was seen alive she was getting into my car at West Winds and departing with me. "Yes, officer, I saw her leaving at about half-past eleven. She was with Godfrey, her new gentleman friend. They left in his car. No, I didn't see either of them after that." The police would then look at my statement, but what evidence was there to support it? Just my word that I had dropped her off at the farm shortly before midnight. That wasn't evidence! I could imagine the line of questioning:

"Tell us in your own time what happened, Mr Sanderson. There's no hurry. Did you park in a quiet place somewhere with the intention of doing a bit more kissing and cuddling, and did it all go too far? Perhaps she didn't really want that kind of relationship, Mr Sanderson, and rejected your advances. We only have *your* word for it that you and she had sexual intercourse earlier in the evening, just after you had returned from the boat trip to Saltcombe. And although it wasn't your intention to harm her, maybe you just lost control of yourself and killed her..."

Right at this very moment they were probably looking into my past – talking to my ex-wife and daughter. "Was he ever violent, Mrs Sanderson? What kind of man is your ex-husband? Have you ever known him use threatening words or behaviour?" "Good gracious no, Inspector, he was never like that – Godfrey is one of the most gentle men you could ever meet. Of course there were long periods when I didn't see him because he worked away from home a lot with his job, you know."

"What was the reason for your marriage breaking down? Was he having an affair?" "Oh no, nothing like that. We just grew apart from one another and seemed to go more and more our own separate ways. It often happens at our time of life these days, I'm afraid." Then the younger voice of my daughter breaking in: "Dad has always been a wonderful father, I couldn't have had a happier childhood. I know he was away a lot because that was the kind of work he did, but he always had big hugs and kisses and presents for me when he came home." Would they support me with comments like that, or had the splitting up of my marriage led to bitterness and resentment and a couldn't-care-less attitude – "Oh well, if he's got himself into trouble, that's *his* fault...I don't want to have anything more to do with him!" It was depressing to realise that I couldn't predict what my own family would have to say about me, whether their comments would be helpful or a hindrance. The only thing that seemed certain to me was that for want of any other suspect, the police would be trying to build up a case against me and I could do nothing except plead my innocence.

But someone else had evidently wanted to end her life. Someone had a reason to kill her. Who? And why? How could I possibly find the answer to those two questions? I had only known her for a matter of hours – I knew nothing at all of her background or what she had done to please or upset other people. Surely that was the key to the mystery – a motive. Somebody somewhere felt strongly enough about *something* to murder her. And it was probably somebody who knew her. People are very rarely killed by a stranger, the murderer is nearly always a person they know well.

My mind immediately went back to the party at West Winds, for that had been a gathering of people she knew. Did something happen when we were there? My mind tried to concentrate on the events of the evening. If it did, I couldn't think what it was, for Rachel had been with me all the time, we were never out of each other's sight, at least not for long.

Even more puzzling was how she came to be discovered beside the river. The tide had been in when we left the party, which was the reason why we had to make the long ten-mile detour to cover less than a mile back to her home at Skylark Farm. I remember that she said something on the journey: "I've got to go and see to Gin before bedtime," and I asked her if she needed any help. She laughed in response: "No, of course not, Godfrey! I go and check the stable every night. Thanks all the same." When she got out of the car in the darkness, did she firstly go into the house or did she make her way straight to the stable? Could there have been someone waiting in the shadows for her? Nothing seemed to make any sense. The one thought that kept coming back repeatedly into my head was that Rachel was dead and I would never see her again. And if that wasn't bad enough, I knew that the finger of suspicion was pointing at me. There would be more police questioning: "What did you do with the knife that you used to kill her, Mr Sanderson? Did you throw it in the river? We've got underwater divers searching for it at this very moment, and when we find it..." Perhaps the evidence would be more circumstantial, based on the fact that logic told them it couldn't be anybody else *other* than me. "If you plead guilty, Godfrey, maybe the prosecution will accept a charge of manslaughter, because I'm sure you didn't set out with the intention of killing her. If you cooperate with us, we'll do our best for you." And so it would go on, inexorably, because they were completely convinced that they had the right man and wouldn't consider any other possibilities.

I have never been more tempted than I was now simply to disappear, run away, go somewhere as far from this place as I could, change my name and start a new life. I was sure it could be done, and yet what would I achieve except to make my guilt seem even more apparent? After all, people don't run away unless they have something to run away from. The innocent would stand their ground, hoping that the truth would prevail. What was the alternative? Stay in Hill Cottage and wait for the police to come and question me again, this time in greater depth, probably at the nearest police station: "Would you like to have your solicitor present, Mr Sanderson?" Hope that their investigation would produce other suspects. Wait for yet more interminable hours before they return with: "Godfrey Sanderson, I am arresting you on suspicion of the murder of Rachel Summers. You are not obliged to say anything..." and so on.

I decided that I needed someone to speak to, someone who was not part of the village, someone who would be prepared to listen to me.

And then I remembered.

8

I Call On A Neighbour

The doorbell didn't work so I knocked instead. It was an old-fashioned front door with panels of opaque coloured glass, and dark brown paint was peeling off the wood. The outside of the building looked tired and dishevelled, as if it had seen far better days and now wanted to be left alone. I would have assumed that it was abandoned had Rachel not told me it was inhabited, or had I not seen smoke curling out of the chimney, and presently a distant voice called out:

"Who is it?"

I paused before replying because my name would have meant nothing.

"A visitor," I shouted back.

"I don't want any visitors!" the voice responded. It was a man speaking, and he sounded impatient and not very well-mannered.

"But I would like to see the gentleman who lives here," I persisted.

"The gentleman who lives here might not want to see

83

you!" he answered tetchily, and then I heard some whispering for a few moments before he spoke again, this time in a lower voice: "Oh all right, then, let him in."

Footsteps approached the front door from inside the little shanty bungalow and the door opened slowly to reveal a woman's face. She was, I suppose, in her thirties, and dressed in working clothes, but what I noticed in particular was the simple beauty of her face. She had her dark hair tied back from her head and held in a big clasp, but the smoothness of her skin, the shape of her mouth and the expression in her eyes made me stare at her in momentary wonderment.

"Would you care to come in," she said sweetly, "Erwin will see you."

"Thank you."

She stepped back to let me through the door and I entered the hall, which was dark and narrow, its thin prefabricated walls bulging unevenly with dampness and age.

"Follow me," she said, "he's down here."

She closed the front door and led me along the hall to a room at the back where a man was sitting at an artist's easel with a paintbrush in his hand. How can I best describe this odd specimen of humanity? He appeared at a glance to be quite small and insignificant, the sort of man you would hardly look at twice, but if you took a second glance, you saw something of his inner self and it immediately held your attention. There was a forcefulness to his personality, not obvious to begin with, but it was there nevertheless in the sharp, darting expression of his eyes and the determined set of his mouth. His face was clearly ageless, for he would have appeared old when young and young when old, and it was virtually impossible to tell what stage he had reached in life's journey. He was dressed in shabby old clothes and ostentatiously covered in paint.

"Well, what do you want to see me about?" he demanded crossly. "I'm busy."

I stepped into the room and looked at the picture he was painting. It was a study in the nude of a beautiful woman, and there she was, standing beside me.

"What an extraordinarily good artist you are," I said, captivated by it. "The way you've handled the light."

"You can stay! Sit down!" he said. "But I must carry on. Belle, would you mind?"

The woman glanced at me a little shyly and slipped her clothes off, resuming her pose on a wooden stool.

"Belle's my housekeeper," said the man, "and I'm Erwin Graham. Who are you?"

"My name's Godfrey Sanderson," I replied. "I moved into Hill Cottage a few days ago so I'm your new neighbour."

"Delighted to meet you and welcome to this humble dwelling. If I wasn't covered in paint I'd offer to shake your hand. Do you mind?" He gestured to his palette.

"Oh no, please carry on."

Erwin Graham resuming his painting and I watched the delicacy of his brushstrokes.

"I assume you have a reason for calling," he said after a while, "and not just to watch an artist at work."

"As a matter of fact, Mr Graham, I had no idea you *were* an artist," I said.

"Actually I'm not. This is just my whim, my idle fancy."

"Erwin is teasing you," said Belle from her position on the stool. "He has been an artist all his life."

"But still seeking recognition!" he said dramatically. "Still seeking recognition! What do you think, Mr Sanderson? Have I captured the essence of Belle's fragile and somehow tragic beauty?"

"Without any doubt I would say it is one of the best paintings I have ever seen," I said. "Where do you usually exhibit?"

"Tate Modern's not interested," he snorted in contempt. "Can you believe it?" Suddenly his attitude changed and he became quieter and less extrovert. "I think it's time I finished for today. Belle, put your clothes back on and get us some coffee, would you, please."

Belle slid obligingly off her stool and slipped her clothes back on, somewhat to my relief.

"I think you'd better call me Erwin," he said, putting his brush in a glass jar to clean it. "And I'll call you Godfrey. Sit down over there. I suppose you've come to see me because you're in trouble."

I blinked in astonishment.

"How did you know?" I asked incredulously, settling down in a sagging armchair which creaked and groaned ominously under my weight.

"Oh, come now, Godfrey – I might live in little more than a broken-down old tin shack, but I do know what's going on around here!" He laughed and leaned forward to pat me on the shoulder. "I'm not quite the eccentric I may appear to be, although some of the good people of Watersford will undoubtedly disagree. Tell me, are you about to be arrested by the police?"

I took a deep sigh.

"Yes, I'm afraid this *is* what's going to happen," I said.

"And clearly you didn't do it otherwise you wouldn't have come to see me. This is a visit in desperation."

I nodded miserably.

"Very much so. I just wanted to talk to someone about it, but not anyone from Watersford. Rachel told me you were an outsider."

"I am. My name might not mean anything to you but I used to work in Fleet Street. I was a chief crime reporter, and perhaps I still would be today if I hadn't cracked up under the strain. It happens in any stressful job, I suppose, but I couldn't take any more of it and dropped out of what we call 'society'. Are you interested to hear more? Well, I spent several weeks sleeping rough on the streets of London – or, more accurately, under various bridges – and then I decided to head in the direction of Totnes because I heard that that is where a lot of people who have – how shall I put it – adopted an alternative way of living have chosen to settle. I arrived in Totnes two years ago and joined the artistic community – painters, writers, musicians. I started painting, and selling my pictures through an art gallery in the town. Still do, in fact. Then, travelling around a bit, I found this place, empty and ramshackle, and moved in. The owners had given up on it so it came into my possession." He gave a little self-satisfied smirk. "The word 'squat' comes to mind, but actually I'm doing them a favour."

At that moment Belle entered the room carrying a tray containing three cups and saucers, a coffee pot filled with steaming black coffee, a milk jug and sugar bowl and put the tray down on a small table.

"Help yourself," she said.

"Thank you," I replied, and took what I wanted.

"Belle comes from a very distinguished line of gipsies," explained Erwin, "but I persuaded her to forsake the travelling life and become my housekeeper." They exchanged smiles in a way that only a couple do, so the word "housekeeper" was plainly a euphemism. She poured his coffee for him because he had paint on his hands and then did the third one for herself, perching back on the stool. "That's my side of the story," he said, looking at me. "Now let's hear yours."

I explained in great detail the events of the last few days and they both listened carefully to everything I had to tell them. When I had finished I sank back in the armchair, momentarily disconcerted by having a spring poke against my backside.

Erwin stroked his chin thoughtfully and remained silent for a while.

"Well," he said at last, "it seems that we have quite a

mystery on our hands. My word, this takes me back to my days of reporting! What a story! A classic!"

"It's a bit more than that," I pointed out to him. "It's my freedom, too, as well as getting to the bottom of what really happened."

"Yes, I know," he said quietly. Suddenly he came fully to life. "Belle, my love, there's work to do! Fetch me my deerstalker and magnifying glass!" He noticed my vexed look and laughed. "Don't worry, it's only our sense of humour. Belle and I have a special understanding of each other."

That was quite obviously the case. I wondered if I had done the right thing, confiding my troubles in this rather peculiar individual, but Erwin Graham seemed to represent my last hope – there was no one else to turn to. Perhaps he sensed my discomfort, for a sudden change came over him and he adopted a serious voice.

"Let's go for a walk," he suggested. "I can think about it much better when I'm out in the fresh air. You've given me all the details but I need more than that. I want to visit the scene of the crime and view it for myself. It might surprise you that I haven't done so already, but I felt I had turned my back on that sort of thing. But now you're here, it's different. Wait a few minutes whilst I clean all this paint off my hands and change my clothes."

Five minutes later he reappeared, looking much tidier, and told Belle that we were going for a little stroll down the lane. We set off together in the direction of the tidal road, passing Hill Cottage on the way. From there, we continued along the lane for another half a mile at which point the path went steeply downhill until it joined the tidal road. We had chosen a good time of day because the tide was out and the mudflats were fully exposed. All signs of police activity had gone and it seemed as if nothing had ever happened to disturb the peaceful tranquillity of Watersford.

"Do you know where the body was found?" asked Erwin.

"Not exactly, I can only show you the approximate place where the police tent was put up," I answered. "I saw them from the bridge, and I could tell that its position was roughly over there." I pointed to the road about a hundred yards from where we were standing, near to a bend.

"Let's go and take a closer look." Then he gave me a sideways glance. "Are you all right to do so?"

I nodded.

"Yes, I'll be fine. I've got over the shock of it now. I feel more a sense of anger than anything. Anger that she should have died in such a horrible way." I shuddered at the thought. "And I feel a sense of guilt, too, because she was with me before it happened. I feel I'm responsible for letting her down and not being there to stop her from being attacked. Was there something I could have done to prevent it?"

"Recriminations are understandable, but you can't blame yourself," said Erwin. "It's only natural to do so, of course," he added.

We arrived at the spot that I had indicated, and a scrutiny of the mud at the side of the road quickly led us to concentrate our attention on a place where the surface of the mud had been disturbed. There had been several incoming tides since the murder, but there was still a noticeable impression in the mud that had not been obliterated by the flowing river water. There were a lot of footmarks, too, from the investigators.

"A very difficult murder scene," said Erwin, and I knew he was talking from experience. "Usually the place where a crime is committed can be preserved for a considerable period giving detectives plenty of time to search for clues and ordinarily we wouldn't be able to get anywhere near it for days, but this is different. Whoever did it must have known how to cover their tracks. And once the tide went out, leaving the body exposed, the police would only have a limited amount of time to collect any evidence before the water came back in again. The tide is not exactly the sort of thing you can do anything to stop." He paced up and down thoughtfully and then turned to me. "What time did you last see Rachel?"

"I dropped her back at the farm at ten to midnight."

"And at what time did you say her body was discovered? Six o'clock the following morning?"

"Yes."

"So we know she died between midnight and six o'clock. What time was high water?"

"I seem to remember somebody mentioning quarter-past one when we went out in the boat."

"Ah yes, you said you went for a trip along the river, didn't you?"

"What are you thinking, Erwin?" I asked.

Erwin Graham pursed his lips, deep in thought.

"I'm thinking," he said slowly, "that her body must have been dumped there during the hours of darkness when the tide was still well in, probably not very long after you last saw her. You told me that her parents said her bed hadn't been slept in, so it's not as if she was awoken in the middle of the night. Anyway, it's getting light at around five o'clock, and I don't think the murderer would have taken the risk of being seen, because even at that hour there's quite a bit of early traffic up and down the tidal road."

"But wait a minute, if it had happened *before* five o'clock, when the road would still have been flooded, it couldn't have been possible to drive a car along there. That means that the murderer was on foot."

Erwin rubbed his chin slowly.

"Yes, it does, doesn't it," he said slowly. "I think we need to get hold of a tide timetable." He continued studying the depression in the mud for a few minutes, looking at it from various angles. Then he glanced up at me and said: "All right, Godfrey, let's carry on walking."

We set off again along the tidal road, heading away from Watersford and towards West Winds. Most of the small boats were now high and dry on sandbanks in the middle of the river. It was an idyllic view, and hard to reconcile with the thought of Rachel lying dead in the mud at the place we had just left.

"If we accept the possibility that *anybody* could have killed her," mused Erwin, "I think we must nevertheless concentrate on those who knew her best of all, including everyone present at the party you both attended. Therefore we shall dismiss the wider world and look only at her closest friends and acquaintances."

"Do you think the party had anything to do with it?" I said in surprise.

"Not necessarily the *party,* but quite possibly one of the people who were there."

"That includes me," I reminded him.

"Present company excepted," said Erwin with a deprecating smile. "I've already ruled you out. So who does that leave? Going on what you told me earlier, it leaves Mr and Mrs Seabourne and their son Jeremy and daughter Catherine, Jeremy's fiancée Emma, Robert Fairweather, James and Julie Carvell and Mr Seabourne's friend George Bland. Is that all?"

I was impressed by Erwin's ability to recall all of their names, but it was probably part of his journalistic training.

"There were a few other people at the house, but I think you've covered the inner circle. From what I could gather, the others were mostly casual acquaintances."

"All right, well in that case the inner circle, as you call it, gives us nine people. Nine suspects who need to be looked into. I say, it's a bit like a classic Agatha Christie whodunit, isn't it? She used to live not far from here, you

93

know."

"Well if she were still alive perhaps she could have come and solved it for us," I remarked flippantly, "or sent Poirot."

"Unfortunately real life doesn't work quite like the pages of fiction." We walked on in silence for a few minutes. Then Erwin said: "Are the police following the same line of thinking as us? Possibly. But if they are working on the theory that it's *you*, I doubt it very much. We've got the field to ourselves."

"But probably not much time to explore it," I responded pessimistically.

"Godfrey, they are not likely to arrest *me*," said Erwin. "Therefore the investigation continues, even in your absence."

I smiled with relief.

"Anyway, we're wasting time," he said, "talking like that. What we need to be doing is looking into how well each of those nine people knew Rachel. That is hardly a task you can undertake yourself because they are not going to talk to you if they think you had anything to do with her death. You will have to leave that to me, and I will report everything I find out from them back to you. In that way it will not arouse the suspicions of at least eight of them, because we are working on the assumption that *one* of the nine is the murderer. Do you agree?"

"That seems a fair assessment," I said. "But won't you be taking a big risk?"

"Of bringing myself to the attention of the one who *is*

the murderer?" said Erwin, and shook his head. "Not the way I intend doing it."

We had reached the point where the tidal road began to go uphill, near the entrance to West Winds, and stopped to look down the estuary. A small cabin cruiser was partly visible through the trees, grounded on a shingle bank. I drew Erwin's attention to it.

"There's the *Sarah Jane*," I told him. "That's the boat we were on the night before last. Actually, I have a feeling that there might once have been something between Rachel and Jeremy, you know. I sensed it a few times at the pub and on the boat – one or two words spoken here and there, a certain look."

"Good, that gives me somewhere to start," said Erwin. "I'll keep notes and show them to you at the end of each day. Either I'll come to your place, or you come to mine. But I don't think we should be seen together from now on. Let's head back to Watersford."

9

The Investigation Begins

Erwin decided that the best way to begin his investigation was by delving into Rachel Summers's past, particularly in relation to the nine people whom I had named as the "inner circle" of the house-party. My idea that Rachel may have had a previous relationship with Jeremy Seabourne was an important lead and one that he felt needed to be looked into, but his first approach was to Catherine Seabourne, Jeremy's sister, because she was Rachel's close friend. I had told him that Catherine worked for a solicitor's in the main street of Kingsbridge, so it did not take him long to find her. It was the second firm of lawyers that he went to. She was one of the junior partners. The receptionist did her best to put him off, but he insisted on seeing her, and in the end they arranged for him to call back at one o'clock, when Miss Seabourne was due to take a break for lunch.

She was somewhat irritated, to say the least of it, when Erwin returned at the appointed time. She came out of her office with an impatient look on her face.

"I don't usually see clients in this way," she informed him coldly.

"I'm not a client," said Erwin.

"Oh, but I understood..."

"Miss Seabourne, I'm a reporter." Of course, there was an element of incorrectness in this statement, for it was more than two years since he had last worked in that capacity and in the meantime he had been little more than an itinerant and an artistic layabout, but old habits die hard so there he was, a working member of the press again. A freelance, if necessary. "Belle would be proud of me if she could see me now!" he told me later. As it happens, in the days when he really was a journalist, Erwin spent much of his time pretending to be something else, but now that he *was* something else, here he was, trying to convince this young woman that he was a reporter.

"What? A journalist?"

"Don't look so surprised, Miss Seabourne. I'm writing an article about the murder of Rachel Summers, and I've been told you were a close friend of hers. But this is not a very good place to talk – could we go somewhere more private?"

"Why should I want to speak to a journalist about it?" she demanded, and he sensed that she was losing her temper. "How dare you come here to my office!" This, he felt, was not a good reaction from someone who worked as a lawyer, for they should remain calm in all circumstances. But he'd had that effect on people many

97

times in the past – it's a sign that you're doing the job properly.

"I'm asking you to speak to me because the young lady is dead and you knew her," said Erwin in a calm, steady voice. "Can you think of a better reason?"

"Oh – very well! But I can't spare much time. Come in my office."

He followed Catherine Seabourne into her small office and sat down by her desk. She remained standing. Being a junior partner, she had one of the less impressive rooms, with a small window that looked out over the back of the building.

"Miss Seabourne, if you don't mind my saying so, you seem to be behaving in rather an offhand way, considering Rachel was one of your friends. Aren't you upset by her death?"

Catherine Seabourne's colour flared up and she spoke in a furious voice: "Of course I'm upset! But I resent your intrusion! How dare you come and question me about this whole tragic business in my working hours! It's completely unacceptable!"

Erwin remained silent for a few seconds, fixing her with an unblinking stare.

"Would you be adopting the same attitude if I had said I was a police officer?" he asked.

She sighed and slowly began to calm down.

"I have already spoken to the police, naturally," she said. "Look, I'm sorry I got rather cross, but when something like this happens, you just want to shut yourself away from the outside world."

"Miss Seabourne, I'm a crime reporter – I only work on serious cases, so I know exactly how you feel. It's not a nice job, asking people what they know about a deceased person in these circumstances, but there are still questions that need to be asked."

She nodded and sat down behind her desk. The fury had subsided, leaving a young woman who looked tired and vulnerable.

"All right," she said quietly, "what *is* it you want to know?"

He slipped a notebook out of his pocket and held a pencil at the ready.

"The only thing I know about Rachel Summers so far is that she was a farmer's daughter aged twenty-six." He gave a rueful smile. "That's not a lot to go on. It tells me nothing about Rachel herself, what sort of girl she was, what she did with her life, whether she was popular and had a lot of friends. Had you known her long yourself?"

Catherine Seabourne nodded. "Yes, Rachel and I had been friends since we were very young. We both went to the same private school and we used to play together in the school holidays. I suppose you'd say we were best friends. I often went to the farm or she came to my home. I got on well with her parents and she got on well with mine, in spite of the fact that there was a big difference in our families' backgrounds. Oh, the Summers family was quite well to do, they weren't poor or anything like that, but the Seabournes were very wealthy with a degree of affluence that made us stand out from most other people in the village, and that is still the case – I'm not being boastful, it's a matter of fact. But to two young girls, it didn't mean anything and I enjoyed my time playing with her at Skylark Farm as much as she enjoyed herself at West Winds. Children are like that, though, aren't they? They don't care, as long as they're having fun. And we did used to have fun. I remember trying to learn how to ride a horse at her farm, but somehow I wasn't very good at it and fell off a few times. Rachel, of course, was brilliant on horseback, she used to compete in show-jumping trials at the local gymkhana and won quite a lot of trophies. When we got older and our lives took us in different directions, we still stayed in touch. I went off to university and she did a business studies course in one of the local colleges. It all seems such a long time ago now, and yet it isn't really."

"Her death must have come as a great shock to you."

"Obviously it did. It's not as if she just dropped dead from some horrible disease or illness – that would have been enough of a shock in itself. But to be *murdered*. I mean, it's just so hard to think of it happening to someone you know."

"And in such a quiet remote village. Can you think of any reason why she *should* have been murdered?"

"None whatsoever. I don't know whether anyone has already told you, but Rachel was at a party which was held at my parents' house the evening before she died."

"I have already been told that," said Erwin. "Is it

possible that the two were connected?"

"Well, are you also aware that she was in the company of a man at the party?"

"What man?"

"Her new gentleman friend Godfrey Sanderson. Really, I'm most surprised if you didn't know that, Mr...Mr – what *is* your name?"

"Erwin Graham. The name of Mr Sanderson has been brought to my attention, but I gathered that he only knew her very slightly."

"So does that rule him out, in your opinion?"

"Miss Seabourne, I'm not in a position to judge the man's innocence or guilt in the matter, since I have no idea whether the police have found any evidence against him. But surely a young woman like Rachel Summers must have had plenty of previous boyfriends, long before this man Godfrey Sanderson turned up in the village and got to know her. He is, I understand, a recent newcomer to the district, and is therefore unlikely to have known her before his arrival here. Perhaps I could come straight to the point by saying that I have been told Rachel was, at one time, friendly with your brother Jeremy."

Catherine Seabourne went quiet for several moments.

"Yes," she said at last, "Jeremy and Rachel were once engaged to be married."

"Engaged to be married?" repeated Erwin, staring at her.

"Mr Graham, lots of people break off engagements without resorting to murder!"

"And lots of people also succumb to jealousy, Miss Seabourne."

"Jeremy? Jealous?" Catherine Seabourne began to laugh. "I suppose at least that proves that you've never met him! Jeremy is one of the most feckless, irresponsible people around! And the fact that he's my brother doesn't prevent me from saying it. All Jeremy wants to do is work as little as possible and have a good time, and he seems to think that the family fortune can provide him with the opportunity to idle his way through life."

"You almost sound disapproving, Miss Seabourne," he said with a faint smile.

Her lips puckered slightly and she shook her head. There seemed to be tears forming in her eyes.

"Why was the engagement broken off?"

"They weren't suited to each other, I suppose. Rachel was attracted in the beginning by Jeremy's attitude to life – fast cars, drinking too much, partying. He's got a flat in London and she used to travel up to see him and stay over for a few nights. They announced their engagement while I was away in university, so I didn't know much about it at the time that it happened. Whenever they were in London they'd go to night clubs and be out until the early hours, but at heart Rachel wasn't that sort. How can I put it? She was mesmerised by Jeremy's personality, as many other people are. But in the end she could see it wasn't leading anywhere. She was a practical country girl, you see, and once all the glitz and glamour of the city wore off, the truth is that she loved nothing better than being on the farm, working in The Skipper's Inn and looking after Gin, her beloved horse."

"You said she got on with your parents. What did they think of her, considering that she was once their prospective daughter-in-law?"

"My mother and father adored her, as everyone else did, and almost looked upon her as one of the family anyway."

"They must be very upset about it themselves."

"Oh they are! My father is terribly distraught, I don't think I've ever seen him look so dreadful. The shock of it has hit him very badly."

"And Jeremy? How has he taken it?"

"Like everyone else – can't believe it's happened."

"Who else was at your parents' party the other night?"

Catherine Seabourne paused to think.

"The usual crowd of friends. Let me see, Emma was there – she's Jeremy's latest girlfriend. James and Julie were there – they came out on the *Sarah Jane* with us."

"James and Julie?"

"James and Julie Carvell. James's family has known ours for years so they usually come over when we've got something on. His parents were there, too. Julie's a nice enough girl, but she's a bit of a quiet little mouse. They haven't been married very long. And George Bland, of course, he was there – he's an old friend and business partner of Daddy's."

"Anybody else?"

"Oh yes, there were quite a few others, I can't name

every one of them."

"And did they all go out on the boat? It must have been quite an excursion."

Catherine Seabourne laughed.

"Good heavens no! We wouldn't all have got on board, I shouldn't think! It was mostly us young people. And I forgot to mention Robert Fairweather, he was at the party, too, and came out on the boat."

"Robert Fairweather," repeated Erwin, noting down the name.

"Robert's so funny, he's one of these people who gets very intense about anything he's interested in. His favourite subject is wooden boats."

Erwin raised his eyebrows and looked at her questioningly.

"Did you say wooden boats? What do you mean? Model boats?"

"No! Real boats! He works for Wallace's in Saltcombe – it's a boat-building company. Let me explain. The *Sarah Jane* is quite old, so she's made of wood, like boats always used to be, whereas these days they're made with moulded plastic hulls. Well, Robert happens to be mad on wooden boats, like some men are mad on steam engines, I suppose. It's a bit of a thing with him and he goes on and on about it at every opportunity, and bores everyone to death..." She turned away suddenly. "That's an unfortunate way of putting it, I'm sorry."

"Going back to some of these other people," said Erwin quickly, "how did Emma and Rachel get on? You mentioned that Emma is Jeremy's latest girlfriend."

"Yes, and *they're* engaged now! Emma's all right, I like her. I wouldn't mind her as a sister-in-law, though whether they'll ever get married I wouldn't like to say. I mean, people usually just live together these days, don't they?"

"Jeremy must like the idea of marriage if he keeps getting engaged," Erwin pointed out.

"Oh, with Jeremy I think it's a grand gesture and nothing more. To answer your question, as far as I know Rachel and Emma got on all right. They had very little in common except that they were both girlfriends of my brother. That doesn't exactly set them at each other's throat, though, does it?"

"Not necessarily," replied Erwin thoughtfully, "unless Emma saw Rachel as a threat."

"But that's ridiculous! Rachel no longer had any interest in Jeremy, not in *that* way. They remained good friends, and nothing more than that."

"It may not be as ridiculous as you think. Do *you* know what's going on deep down in Emma's mind? Especially if Rachel was still one of the crowd, as you might put it."

"But according to the police, Rachel was attacked with some sort of knife. If you had ever met Emma, you'd never imagine her doing something like that!"

"The word jealousy comes to mind again, Miss Seabourne," said Erwin, and made a careful note of it.

Catherine Seabourne shook her head in disbelief.

"No, no, I'm sorry, I think you're entirely wrong if you

suspect Emma of being involved."

"But we know *somebody* did it, so how do you know that somebody isn't one of Rachel's friends? And all right, you can count Godfrey Sanderson in that same category, if you want to. Nine people, if you exclude yourself."

"Why not include me as well and make it ten! And are you seriously suggesting that my parents should be listed among the suspects?"

Erwin Graham laid his pencil down on the notebook and looked gravely into Catherine Seabourne's eyes. An expression of hostility had returned to her face, but there was doubt in it, too.

"Miss Seabourne, *you* may know you didn't do it, but you cannot say that for anyone else, including your parents or your brother. Your friend Rachel Summers is dead, horribly murdered, that you *do* know. And the culprit is somewhere around here. As to the identity of the culprit – at the moment, *nobody* knows. And because we don't yet know *why* she died, I suggest you take great care from now on."

"You don't mean...?" she began, and her voice trailed off to nothing.

"I mean simply this – be cautious. It seems to me, Miss Seabourne, that the police are intent on concentrating their inquiries into Rachel Summers's last known movements and that suggests that they regard Godfrey Sanderson as their chief suspect. Personally, I think they should be looking elsewhere. If I am right and they are wrong, that means the perpetrator of this dreadful murder is from the locality, and in the absence of a motive it seems sensible to exercise every reasonable precaution."

"Mr Graham, I know my family and friends far better than I know this man Mr Sanderson, and yet you are seriously asking me to consider the possibility that one of *them* has killed poor Rachel and not *him*. But we already know that he was the last person she was with – I even saw them leave our house together! Your suggestion defies all logic. And what does it matter if she had only just met him? For all we know, he may have done the same thing before in another part of the country!"

"You could be right," said Erwin, without sounding convinced. "What time did the party end?"

"It went on until about one o'clock in the morning, but I'd gone up to bed by then. I seem to remember that some of the guests were leaving when we got back to the house after going out in the boat. Robert Fairweather left at about that time, then Rachel and Godfrey and the Carvells followed at about half-past eleven. Several of the guests stayed the night, as they often do."

"Jeremy and Emma?"

"I can't remember, but I imagine they stayed the night, they usually do."

"So various people left at different times or stayed at the house overnight?"

"Yes, that's about it. I didn't take much notice who did exactly what and when because it's not the sort of thing one usually does at a party!"

"And if you retired to bed for the night before the party had ended, presumably you weren't there to see who did what and when."

"Those who were still talking and drinking when I went upstairs to bed are those who stayed the night," said Catherine in exasperation.

"Including Jeremy and Emma?"

"Yes!"

"Even though you're not sure whether they did stay the night?"

"I said I couldn't remember if they did or not! Really, this is worse than a police interrogation!"

Erwin smiled and shook his head.

"Well, thank you, Miss Seabourne, you've been most helpful, but there is one last thing I'd like to ask you, if you wouldn't mind. How can I get in touch with all the others? I'd very much like to speak to each of them so that I can obtain as much information as possible about Rachel. Do you think they would agree to talk to me?"

"On the strength of what you've put me through, they'd be well advised not to!"

Erwin took a deep breath.

"I'm serious, Miss Seabourne."

She looked a bit dubious.

"I'm not sure about Jeremy or my father," she replied slowly with a frown, and then her expression suddenly cleared, as though the thought had crossed her mind that any reluctance on their part might be misinterpreted. "Actually, I don't see why not. I live with my parents at

West Winds on the tidal road and so does Jeremy when he's not in London, but his movements are very erratic – you never know where he is from one day to the next. George Bland is staying with us at the moment, and as for James and Julie Carvell, Emma Richmond and Robert Fairweather, I'll write their addresses down for you." She picked up a pen from her desk and scribbled a few lines on a small jotter. "Emma lives with her mum here in Kingsbridge, the others all live and work in Saltcombe," she explained as she was writing. She tore off the little sheet of paper and handed it to Erwin, who glanced down at it and saw three addresses written in neat handwriting.

"Thank you for taking the time and trouble to answer my questions, Miss Seabourne, you've been most helpful. Should anything come to mind which you think I ought to know about, this is where I can be contacted." Erwin ripped one of the pages from his notebook with a telephone number on it. He got up to leave, and had the feeling that the young lady was looking very thoughtful and distracted. He wondered if she knew more than she had said.

Erwin's notes on Catherine Seabourne: Twenty-six years of age, very attractive, intelligent, inclined to be quick-tempered. Regarded Rachel as a very close friend. Protective of her brother Jeremy, who sounds irresponsible. Seems very conscious of family's wealth.
Impression – favourable, but I felt she was holding something back.
Possible motive – nothing immediately obvious.

10

The Investigation Continues

The next one on the list that Erwin would particularly liked to have spoken to was Jeremy Seabourne, but his sister had indicated that his whereabouts were uncertain and he may or may not still be at West Winds – he might even have returned to London. Erwin could have made good use of his time by staying in Kingsbridge to find Emma, Jeremy's fiancée, in the hope that she could give him some idea of Jeremy's whereabouts, but somehow he felt it was too soon to question her. However, there was an irresistible temptation to track her down if only to see what she looked like.

He pulled out the piece of paper that Catherine Seabourne had given him in her office and noticed that she had written down a telephone number for Emma Richmond as well as her home address. Not being in possession of a mobile phone, he found a public telephone box and dialled the number. After a few seconds it was answered by a woman's voice.

"Hello?" she said. It did not sound like the voice of a

young woman and Erwin guessed that it was Emma's mother.

"Hello, may I speak to Emma, please," he responded, hoping that Miss Richmond would not be there.

"I'm sorry, she won't be home until later, she's at work. Can I take a message?"

"No thanks, I just wanted to have a quick word with her. Do you think she'd mind if I rang her at work?"

"I don't know," said the woman, suddenly sounding doubtful. "Who is it speaking, please?"

"Oh, just one of Jeremy's friends," said Erwin casually, and decided to take a chance. "I'm trying to get hold of him, and Emma probably knows where he is."

"Have you got her office number?" asked her mother.

"No," he replied, "I'm not even sure where she works."

Her mother gave him the name of an estate agent's office in the town followed by its telephone number, but the name was quite sufficient. He thanked her very much, and less than a minute after stepping out of the telephone box he was standing outside the estate agent's window, supposedly looking at properties for sale. Through the window he could see several desks spread around the office. The one nearest the window was unoccupied, but two desks further back had young women sitting behind them. One was on the telephone, the other was sorting through paperwork. Which one was Emma, he wondered? He was now a little unsure what to do. Should he go inside the office and ask to speak to her?

Erwin carried on studying the properties for sale in the

window whilst he made up his mind how to proceed. In the end, he decided that it was too good an opportunity to miss.

He opened the door and went in. The young woman on the telephone continued with her conversation, merely glancing at him in a cursory way, but her colleague, the one going through the list of particulars, gave him a friendly smile.

"Can I help you?" she asked brightly.

Erwin smiled back and pointed towards the rows of property details displayed on the wall.

"Just having a look," he said, and she nodded.

He made it his business to read every one they had, taking his time to do so. The telephone conversation came to an end and he listened carefully to the occasional remarks between the two young women as they continued with their work in case a name was mentioned, but it wasn't. When he felt he could hardly spend any more time reading through the houses for sale, Erwin made up his mind to take a direct approach. He turned and said: "Which one of you is Emma?"

"Neither of us," said the one who had already spoken to him. "Emma's out on a viewing appointment. I'm Karen and that's Robyn over there."

"Oh, sorry. I spoke to Emma on the phone a week or so ago, that's all." It seemed a harmless enough little lie.

"She should be back by half-past three if you want to speak to her, unless one of us can help."

"It's Emma I really wanted to see," he said

apologetically. "I'll call back later."

Erwin left the office and noticed a small cafe up the street. Five minutes later he was sitting at a corner table by the window, drinking a cup of tea. From his table he had a good view down Fore Street. The time went very slowly and after half an hour he found himself draining the teapot. Half-past three came and went, but eventually he saw a young woman, smartly dressed in a dark blue business suit and wearing high-heeled shoes, her long dark hair tied back in a ponytail, going into the estate agent's office. He made his way back down the hill and sure enough, the same young woman was now sitting behind the desk near the window. He entered the office and went straight up to her. Robyn was on the telephone again and Karen had her back turned to him, looking for something in a filing cabinet at the far end of the office.

"Emma?" he said, sitting in a chair on the client's side of her desk.

"Yes," replied the young woman with a friendly smile. Erwin could see that she matched Godfrey's description of her, though she was more attractive than he had imagined. Perhaps it was the pleasing smile, which seemed genuine rather than the automatic response, the perfunctory act as it were, required by her occupation.

He lowered his voice to suggest that the matter was confidential.

"I wanted to get in touch with Jeremy," he explained, trying to say it in a tone of familiarity, "and I thought you might know where he is at the moment." No need to tell her why, he thought, just make it sound casual.

"Oh, he's gone back to London," she said. "He was home for the weekend, but he went yesterday because he had to take a car back. Is it anything urgent?"

"No," replied Erwin. "It's all right, I'll see him when he's home again. Do you have any idea when that might be?"

She giggled. "Next weekend, I hope. It's my birthday!"

An idea suddenly crossed Erwin's mind, for although he had not intended to speak to her at this stage in the inquiry, it now seemed too good an opportunity to miss – the circumstances would not present themselves again. If Jeremy were now out of the area, Erwin had a perfectly good reason to speak openly to his fiancée.

"Could you spare me a few minutes of your time?" he asked, and leaned forward. "It's about Rachel."

Emma's eyes widened. "Oh."

"Perhaps we could talk somewhere more quietly. There's a cafe across the road or we could go and sit by the quayside."

She thought for a moment and looked down at her small gold wristwatch. It was neat and dainty, like her.

"Karen," she said, turning in her seat, "I've got to pop out with this gentleman for ten minutes. Would you mind answering my phone calls and taking any messages? I'm expecting to hear from Mr Percival with his response to an offer. Thanks."

They left the office and stepped out into the street.

"Let's go down to the quay," she suggested. "I sit at my

114

desk drinking coffee all day when I'm not showing clients around houses, so it's nice to get some fresh air."

Kingsbridge is situated five miles inland from the coast, and the estuary ends in a natural open harbour, with boats tied up against shallow stone walls that extend for quite a long distance along two opposite embankments. The tide was fully in and the boats were riding high. Erwin and Emma found an empty seat overlooking the water and sat down. People walked past without paying any attention to the small nondescript middle-aged man sitting beside a smartly-dressed and attractive young woman; many of them looked like tourists. Gulls circled overhead, uttering their mournful cries.

"Are you from the police?" asked Emma, staring closely at Erwin.

He smiled and shook his head.

"Do I look like a policeman?" he said, gesturing to himself. He could hardly look less like an officer of the law.

She laughed.

"No, not really." She tried again. "Are you a friend of Jeremy's?"

He sighed. "I'd like to say yes, but that would be untruthful and I'd never forgive myself for lying to a young lady like you. I'm a crime reporter." He very conveniently ignored the fact that he was lying anyway.

"Oh!"

"You sound surprised."

"Well I am a bit, although I suppose I shouldn't be.

Why do you want to speak to me?"

"To find out how well you knew Rachel."

Emma stared towards the water and seemed to go into a trance, but Erwin knew she was thinking. He felt she didn't know where to begin.

"And before you answer," he said softly, "may I offer you my condolences on losing a friend in such a terrible way, but perhaps I could add my congratulations on your engagement." He was looking at the sapphire ring on her finger.

"Thank you," she replied with a fleeting smile. At length she gathered her thoughts. "I met Jeremy at a party almost a year ago and I thought he was the most handsome, dashing young man I had ever set my eyes on. He still is my knight in shining armour, as they say. It seems that I caught his eye, too, and we started going out together. I quickly got to know his friends, including Rachel, and it wasn't long before I discovered they had once been engaged. Jeremy saw nothing wrong with having his ex-fiancée in the background because that's the way he is. So of course I got to know her."

"Did you mind her presence?"

"Quite honestly I would rather she hadn't been there because I felt, to begin with, that I was in the company of my rival. But I got used to it after a while, and once I could see there was nothing between them any more, I came to regard her as a good friend. She was also very friendly with Jeremy's sister Catherine so I accepted her as part of the family circle. You can't go through life

116

harbouring jealousy, can you?"

"I'm afraid some people do," said Erwin, "but go on."

Emma shrugged her shoulders. "There's nothing more to say. Jeremy and I had decided to share our lives together, so we got on with planning our future."

"What does he do for a living?" he asked. Godfrey had indicated that he did very little.

"He works for George Bland, selling cars in the West End. Expensive ones, like Aston Martins, Ferraris and Porsches," said Emma. "He often brings one down when he comes home and then takes it back again afterwards." She sniggered. "I think he likes showing off in them."

"I don't blame him," said Erwin, "I'm sure I'd be the same. Where are you planning to live when you're married?"

"We're staying here in Devon. It doesn't take him long to travel up and down on the motorway."

"Nice job to have – it seems to give him plenty of spare time."

"Oh yes, he only needs to sell one or two cars a week."

Erwin smiled indulgently and gazed out over the rippling water of the creek, watching it lapping against the boats tied up on the opposite side.

"How did you take the news of Rachel's death?" he asked.

"I couldn't believe it, I was completely horrified," said Emma, turning to look at him with a troubled frown. "It seemed so *unreal*, to think that someone you know has been murdered. But although I know it's a perfectly beastly thing to say, in a way I felt a *tiny* bit relieved."

"That she was no longer able to come between you and Jeremy?"

"Yes!"

"But was that ever likely? You said yourself that there was nothing between them any more."

"I know I said that – but it's still in the back of your mind, isn't it? You keep wondering."

"I'm told that she'd recently started seeing an older man," said Erwin, without mentioning Godfrey's name.

Emma nodded.

"Yes, I know, there are rumours that she liked older men," she said, and then, after a pause, she went on, "and there are also rumours going around that she had a miscarriage several months ago."

"But you don't know whose it was?"

"No! That's my point! There were so many things about Rachel you didn't know. It might have been Jeremy's!"

"Do you have any idea who may have had a reason to kill her?" asked Erwin.

"Good gracious, no! Perhaps it was a madman."

"There's an opinion that it could have been Godfrey Sanderson, the man she was seeing."

Emma stared at him for a moment.

"Why? What reason would he have to murder her? I don't think she'd be the sort to reject his advances!"

"I imagine that's the motive the police are working on, nevertheless."

"But I saw them together and they were *happy*. And believe me, so was I! That's not the stage in a romance when you go around murdering your partner, and if that's what the police think, I'm sure they're hopelessly wrong."

"When you saw them together, was that at the party in the Seabournes' house?"

"Yes. We also went out on the river in the family's boat. There was even champagne on board – it was very nice."

"Where did you go?"

"Down to Saltcombe and back. It was a lovely evening."

"And when the party was over? What happened then?"

"Some people went home, others stayed overnight at the house."

"What did you do?"

Emma hesitated.

"I stayed."

"Let me put this question to you, Miss Richmond – could the murderer be one of her friends, do you think?"

"One of her *friends?* Why would one of her friends want to kill her?"

"It's entirely logical. Most people are murdered by the hand of someone they know and very often trust," Erwin pointed out. "Are you telling me there isn't one of her friends who might have thought of killing her at one time or another?"

Emma looked away.

"You're right, of course. Even *I* had dark thoughts

about her. But it didn't go any further than that! You might have bad thoughts about someone – only that's as far as it goes!"

"And yet Rachel is dead, so the bad thoughts must have gone deeper in somebody's mind," surmised Erwin thoughtfully. "Anyway, Miss Richmond, you must be getting back to your office, I've taken up quite enough of your time. Mr Percival might be ringing with his response to the offer, whatever that might be. Thank you very much for giving me your point of view. I shall try and speak to Jeremy when he's next home."

"I haven't said anything that can be held against me, have I?" she asked anxiously. "You must understand, in spite of what I've told you, that I wish so much that it hadn't happened. I want to see Rachel alive again!" And she began to cry. "I'm sorry," she sobbed, "but I feel sad in one way and glad in another – and I shouldn't be feeling like this!"

She dried her eyes and gave a bleary smile.

"Life can be so awful, can't it?" she said.

Erwin drew a deep breath and looked across the water again. "Yes, Miss Richmond," he said, "I'm afraid it can."

Erwin's notes on Emma Richmond: Mid-twenties, winningly attractive, articulate and emotional. A sensitive young woman who feels deeply about her relationship with Jeremy Seabourne and seems oblivious to his apparently irresponsible ways. I think she has been drawn into a situation for which she is not fully prepared. Her attitude to Rachel Summers is ambivalent, and she has cast Rachel

in a much different light from how I had originally imagined her.
Impression — favourable, I liked her honesty and openness.
Possible motive — jealousy.

11

I Receive A Visitor

There was a knock on the front door of Hill Cottage at seven o'clock in the evening and I got up apprehensively from my seat in the lounge to see who it was. Erwin stood outside. I breathed a sigh of relief.

"I see your car has gone," he said.

"It was taken away this morning for examination," I replied. "The police said I might not get it back for some time."

"Don't be too dismayed about it. If you were the last known person to see Rachel alive, it would be very surprising if they *didn't* take it to look at. From a procedural point of view, it would be carelessness tantamount to dereliction of duty. What else have they got to go on?"

"Nothing, I suppose. Anyway, come in and tell me what you've been doing. Have you had a busy day?"

"Yes, I went to Kingsbridge to see Catherine Seabourne and managed to speak to Emma Richmond as well. Here are the reports." He handed me several sheets of paper on which he had written copious notes, based on his original summaries.

"What did you make of them?" I asked.

"Very much as you described them both, but I thought Emma was prettier than you made her out to be. Catherine Seabourne was not at all pleased to see me when I presented myself at her office, but after getting off to a rather bad-tempered start, she soon calmed down and told me quite a few things, which are all written down in the notes I've given you, but as I said at the end, I felt she was holding back on something. By contrast, Emma was a straightforward and sweet-natured young lady who came across much as I would have expected her to, in the circumstances. She's very mixed up in her mind about it all – one minute she confesses that she's pleased Rachel is dead, the next minute she wishes she wasn't, but you can blame Jeremy for that. He wants everything his own way, and he's forced her to accept the continued presence of Rachel. According to Emma, Rachel had a miscarriage some time ago, and it seems she also liked older men!"

"That's one thing we know is true," I said with a wry smile. "So where does it get us?"

"Not very far," admitted Erwin, "but at least it's a start. If there is any substance in my belief that we need to delve into the background of her friends, I've now had the story from the first two."

"And can you rule either of them out?"

"No, not really. Her best friend gives me the

impression of keeping something back, and her love rival *could* have been overcome by jealousy. What I need to find out now is how many of the others are hiding possible motives."

"But they're all meant to be *friends*," I protested.

"My dear Godfrey," said Erwin with a patient sigh, "take any group of friends you can think of. They regularly meet up in the pub or the club, or they go to the same church, play golf, socialise each weekend or even go on holiday together. How often do you think that wonderful group of friends, seemingly so happy in each other's company, are secretly criticising one another behind their backs and building up resentment over something usually quite trivial? Something that starts off very small, perhaps, but grows in the mind of the malcontent until the pressure becomes too much, causing them to explode in anger! In most instances it's nothing more serious than the end of another beautiful friendship. Do you see what I'm getting at? It's an everyday occurrence!"

"And you think that's happened here?"

"The undercurrents of discontent are already apparent. They exist."

"So what happens next?"

"I think my next move must be to pay a visit to West Winds in order to speak to Mr and Mrs Seabourne, which will also give me a chance to find out if Jeremy is there. If not, he should be back by Friday because it's Emma's birthday on the weekend and he won't be missing that, not if he's got any sense. There's this fellow George Bland, too – I wonder if he's still around? After that, it's off to Saltcombe to find Robert Fairweather and the Carvells, but that shouldn't be too difficult: I'll find him in his boatyard or at his home address and them in their guest house or hotel, whatever it is."

"It means a lot of travelling around for you," I said.

Erwin waved his hand dismissively.

"Once you've spent a few nights aimlessly tramping around the streets of London with nowhere to go, this is nothing!" he declared. "Besides, I have ways and means."

I raised my eyebrows, inviting him to elaborate.

"When I first came to Devon," he explained, "I joined a crowd of people in Totnes who had each decided to give up a lot of things everyone else takes for granted – cars, televisions, all the modern conveniences that people work hard for in order to be able to afford them. That's why I had my breakdown in the first place – because of the relentless ever-increasing pressure to have *more*. So I chose to have *less*, and now I'm as happy as can be. Ask Belle, she'll tell you. Why go to the expense of owning a car when there's a perfectly adequate bus service? Besides," he added with a wink, "I happen to have a good arrangement with Micky who runs the small garage here in Watersford. He keeps a couple of old cars and vans out the back and lets me borrow them if I need to. I give him a painting from time to time in return."

"So you *do* drive around in a car?" I said.

"Yes," confessed Erwin, "I do – except it's not mine."

"Is that how you got to Kingsbridge?"

He nodded.

"I took the little Fiat. It's rusting to bits and the brakes don't work, but it got me there and back."

I laughed.

"It's called making do," he said. "Anyway, back to more important matters. My theory is that if I can get each one of Rachel's friends to talk to me about her, I shall not only discover a great deal about her life but also there's a good chance that certain facts will emerge which either agree with the general narrative or not. I'm interested in the ones that do not."

"Can you explain what you mean?"

"Well, if we work on the assumption that the murderer is one of that group, there will be details that he or she cannot tell me about for the simple reason that to do so would be equivalent to making a confession – therefore those details will be withheld, or twisted into a different version of events. Sooner or later there will be a discrepancy in the stories they are telling me which will point to the culprit. It may not necessarily stand up in a court of law as evidence, but the gathering of evidence will come later and should be the job of the police once we establish the truth of what actually happened."

"I'm putting a lot of faith in you, Erwin," I said.

He gave me a twisted grin.

"I know," he replied, and there were a few moments of silence. "There's not much else to report," he continued. "Belle went into Watersford earlier and said that the talk among the villagers is that the police are completely baffled. Apparently they have yet to find the murder weapon, and that seems to be causing some concern. They did a thorough search of the river on the first day, when they had the advantage of low water, but found nothing."

"Detective Sergeant Hoskins came back earlier when they took my car away," I said. "It seems that a superintendent has been put on the case."

"Did the good sergeant say anything or ask you any more questions?"

"No, he seemed to play the whole thing down, making out that it was routine to examine any vehicles that Rachel had travelled in before her death, not that there are any others."

"That's true enough. If you *had* killed her, they might reasonably expect to find traces of her blood inside the car."

"He also asked to look around the cottage, and spent some time in the kitchen."

"Searching for anything that might resemble the murder weapon, no doubt."

"That's what I thought. There are plenty of knives in the kitchen drawers. Of course, they all belong to the owners of the house, and not to me, but that's hardly the point, though it does raise an interesting technicality – do the police have to speak to the owners before conducting a more formal search?"

"I rather think not. You are legally responsible for what

goes on inside this house during the period of tenancy. Who are the owners, as a matter of interest?"

"Mr and Mrs Harrington, but they live in another part of the country. His mother used to be the owner before she died. They did it up, intending it to be a holiday let. But I managed to arrange a year's rental of it."

The irony of that statement was not lost on Erwin.

"I hope you get to spend the year in it," he remarked. "Do you have your money back if you don't?" He suddenly remembered something he had meant to ask. "Are you well stocked for food? Do you need anything? Because if you want to avoid having to go into the village, Belle can do some shopping for you."

"I'm all right for everything at the moment, thanks. I'll need bread and milk in a couple of days, but it's fine for now."

"Come to us for dinner tomorrow. Seven o'clock. I can then give you the report on Day Two."

12

The Investigation Moves To West Winds

"I'm afraid he's not here. Can I help you?" The tall elegant lady looked down from the front doorstep of West Winds and spoke with dignified self-assurance. Her dark hair was gathered up and tied neatly behind her head and she had an almost hawkish look to her face. She must have been a very good-looking woman in her younger years, but now a distinct touch of severity to those same distinguished features gave her an air of mild middle-aged condescension. This was Minkie Seabourne, the woman whose youthful fancy for mink coats had conferred on her a slightly absurd pet name for the rest of her life.

Erwin Graham's arrival at West Winds and a simple request to see Jeremy Seabourne did not appear to unsettle her in the least, despite offering his credentials as a reporter.

"Would you mind very much if I asked *you* a few questions instead?" he proposed in a manner that suggested why don't we get this rather unpleasant job over and done with?

"Not in the slightest," she replied graciously. "Do come in and we'll go in the lounge. Can I offer you some refreshment, Mr – er – ?"

"Graham."

"Mr Graham. Some people find the morning much too early for a drink, but I can offer you anything you like. Whisky? Cold beer? A glass of wine?"

"A cup of tea would be very nice," he said, walking beside her across the hall and into the lounge, where he was immediately struck by the magnificent view out through the French windows, showing the other side of the estuary which could be clearly seen between the trees in the front garden. The meandering course of the river lay out of sight, obscured by the land in the foreground that formed the sloping garden.

"China or Indian?"

"I beg your pardon?"

"The tea."

"Oh, however it comes," he said accommodatingly.

"Milk or lemon?"

"Milk and no sugar, thank you."

"If you'll excuse me, I'll go and tell my housekeeper. I won't keep you a moment."

Minkie Seabourne detached herself from beside him and disappeared out of the room. Erwin felt quite relieved, for her tall, dominant presence made him appear rather diminutive and he watched her go with the same sense of awe that many men had experienced when standing in close proximity to her. Her footsteps receded across the hall and he found himself wondering if the housekeeper was anything like Belle. He had his doubts. He began studying some of the pictures on the wall by the French windows with the keen critical eye of an artist. As with everything else in the house, they were expensive and quite possibly originals.

"Now then, Mr Graham, do sit down and make yourself comfortable." Mrs Seabourne swept back into the room like a ship in full sail. He seated himself on a velvet-covered chaise longue and she perched delicately at the end of it, crossing one leg over the other. "What sort of questions were you thinking of asking?"

"About Rachel Summers."

"Ah, of course, poor dear Rachel. What can I say? It's so terribly, terribly tragic for such an awful thing like that to happen to her."

"She was almost one of the family, I've been told."

"Perfectly true, she *was* almost one of the family. I've watched her growing up since she was a little girl of five or six. My daughter Catherine was her best friend, you see, they're practically the same age and they were in school together, sitting next to each other in the classroom."

"I've spoken to Catherine already."

"Oh, have you? Well, I don't really know where to begin, Mr Graham."

"Could I start with your son Jeremy, because he was once engaged to her, was he not?"

Minkie Seabourne's mouth opened momentarily as if

she were going to say something but then changed her mind.

"Yes, he was," she said. "It was such a surprise because Charles and I thought of her as nothing more than Catherine's friend without realising that she and Jeremy had become infatuated with each other. Rachel could so easily have become our daughter-in-law. She was from a farming family in Watersford, you know."

"If you don't mind my asking, what happened to break off the engagement?"

"Oh, differences between them, I suppose," she said, waving her hands vaguely in the air. "Jeremy's a very *delicate* boy, and I think Rachel was a bit too *robust* for him." She made it sound as though Rachel Summers was physically more than a match for Jeremy Seabourne and that he struggled to satisfy her, and perhaps that's the way it was, but Erwin had a suspicion that this was probably a mother's fond view of her son and he doubted if Jeremy could do much wrong in her eyes.

"Were you pleased when they split up?"

Minkie hesitated.

"I thought it was for the best – for everyone."

"Did they remain on friendly terms afterwards?"

"It made no difference at all to Rachel's friendship with Catherine, so naturally she still used to see Jeremy whenever she came to the house to visit her, and they just treated each other as friends. We held a house-party only last Saturday evening and – well, *that* was the night Rachel was murdered, after leaving here, the poor dear thing.

Oh, I feel so *responsible*. If only she'd stayed the night, as she had done so often in the past, it would never have happened."

"Did you see her leave the party?"

"Yes, I did. She came to say goodbye before she left, and to thank me. She was so good at little things like that. She had a gentleman with her and they left together – in his car, I believe."

"This is the man whom the police are treating as a suspect?"

Minkie Seabourne lowered her voice.

"Yes," she said, sounding scandalised. "To think that he was here one minute, accepting our hospitality, and then murdering her the next!"

"Assuming that he did it."

"Well, the police usually have a good idea, don't they?"

"They're not *always* right, Mrs Seabourne. In the meantime, Jeremy has a new fiancée, I understand."

"Yes, Emma. She's a dear little thing and they're *terribly* in love, you know."

"So you expect to be welcoming her into the family soon?"

"Yes." From her manner, Minkie Seabourne seemed to have much more enthusiasm for the prospect of Emma as a daughter-in-law than she did for Rachel. She leaned forward and lowered her voice. "They're getting married next year. We're having a big marquee in the garden." Erwin heard the sound of a tea-tray rattling in the hall and she sat up straight again. The housekeeper, a

133

pleasant-looking woman in her forties, entered the room carrying a large silver tray and set it down on a small table. Her eyes met Erwin's for an instant and she gave him a smile – the same sort of innocently seductive look that Belle was very good at doing – and he noted it with interest. "Thank you, Mrs Brown," murmured Minkie, "Mr Graham takes milk but no sugar."

The housekeeper poured two cups of tea and handed one of them to Erwin. Her fingers brushed lightly against his wrist in doing so, almost accidentally, and she caught his eye for a second time.

"Well, I hope they'll be very happy together," he said, and added quickly, "Jeremy and Emma." He began to drink his tea. "What happened when the party was over?"

Minkie gave him an admonishing look.

"Our parties are never *over*," she said reproachfully, "the word has such an air of finality to it. Quite a few of our guests stay the night with us. It was a *house-party*, you see, Mr Graham, and house-parties go on for the weekend."

"But Rachel and a few others left here late on Saturday evening."

"Not everyone stays."

"So who exactly did leave?"

"Well, Rachel, of course, and her gentleman friend, they left before midnight. So did James and Julie, they had to get back to Saltcombe where they run a guest house. Robert left early, too. But as far as I can remember, most of the others stayed."

"What about Emma? I assume she spent the night here,

134

too."

"Emma? Well I expect she did – she wouldn't want to travel back to Kingsbridge at that time, would she? Mind you, now you come to mention it, I cannot recall seeing her the following morning at breakfast. We always put on a big traditional breakfast for our guests, like they used to in the old days."

"Perhaps she had a lie-in with Jeremy," suggested Erwin. It seemed quite a reasonable supposition, he thought, for a young couple to want to stay together in bed on a Sunday morning for they would have better things to do than think about breakfast, traditional or otherwise.

Minkie Seabourne frowned and shook her head slowly. There was an awkward silence.

"Where do they intend living when they're married?" he inquired hurriedly, changing the subject.

"Jeremy would like to stay here," said Mrs Seabourne. "It's a big house, after all, and there are plenty of rooms. And Emma would have company when he's away, which he is a lot of the time. I expect they'll have children – she looks the sort who won't have any difficulty – and this is such a lovely place to bring up little ones."

"Young couples usually like a place of their own," pointed out Erwin tactfully.

"Young couples usually don't have the opportunity to live in a house like West Winds," came the prim reply, and he laughed.

Suddenly a door at the far end of the lounge opened

and a man walked in from an adjoining room. He stopped when he saw them.

"Oh, I beg your pardon," he said apologetically, "I didn't know we had visitors."

"That's quite all right, George, come in and meet Mr Graham," said Mrs Seabourne. "Mr Graham, this is Mr George Bland, a very old friend of the family who happens to be staying here for a few days. George and my husband have shared business interests."

George Bland seemed reluctant at first to come any further into the room but Minkie Seabourne beckoned firmly with her hand and he stepped forward. Erwin stood up and acknowledged his entrance with a gentle nod of the head and a polite smile.

"We were just talking about dear Rachel," explained Mrs Seabourne. "Mr Graham is a newspaper journalist and he's covering the story of her murder."

For a moment it looked as though George Bland wished to do nothing more than turn around and go straight back out of the room again, but he kept approaching and gave Erwin a stiffly affable smile in return.

"Bad business," he muttered quietly, and Erwin, turning his attention completely to him, wondered if he really meant "bad for business."

"Did you know Rachel well, Mr Bland?" he asked.

"Er, I had met her a few times in the past when I've been here," said Bland rather hesitantly. "Is it relevant whether I knew her well or not?"

"It's not an unreasonable question to ask."

"In that case I would say that I had nothing to do with her whatsoever, and she had nothing to do with me. We both happened to be visitors to the same household, occasionally at the same time, but whereas she spent her time with the children, I spent my time with the adults."

"The children now being adults themselves."

"Quite so, but the generation gap remains."

"And although you have shared probably many hours in the same household together, there's nothing you can tell me about her?"

"I don't think you understand what I'm trying to tell you, Mr Graham – there's nothing I can say that will be of any use to you. We hardly knew one another."

"George is a very private individual," said Minkie in an attempt to come to his rescue. He gave her a look of relief and gratitude.

Erwin Graham turned back to her.

"Is it possible to speak to your husband, Mrs Seabourne? I'd like to ask him his opinion of Rachel."

"I'm afraid Charles isn't here at the moment."

"Can you give me some idea when he might be?"

"He's had to go away for a few days on business."

"And Jeremy – when might I have a chance to see him?"

"He's away from home too, but he should be back by Friday, and quite possibly sooner than that."

Erwin remembered that it would be Emma's birthday on the weekend – perhaps he could contrive some

137

method of seeing Jeremy then.

"Well, thank you very much, Mrs Seabourne, I think I've already taken up more than enough of your time. And thanks for the tea, it was very nice."

"Earl Grey," she said.

Erwin stood up to leave and noticed, in a large mirror over the fireplace, that Minkie Seabourne and George Bland exchanged glances behind his back, Minkie seeming to frown at him while George stared back unblinkingly. By attempting to draw him out with those few ostensibly straightforward questions, Erwin felt that he had briefly penetrated the defences of a man who had something to hide, and for that reason he considered it a successful encounter. On the other hand, Bland would now be on the defensive, and that might prove an awkward obstacle at some later stage. A return to West Winds was undoubtedly necessary, but this strangely self-contained little man might make it difficult if he were still there. In a curious way George Bland seemed to exert a lot of influence, and Erwin somehow felt that his secretiveness was of great significance.

Mrs Seabourne accompanied her visitor to the front door.

"I must apologise for George," she said in a quiet voice once they were out in the hall. "He and my husband have done business together for many years, but they are very different types of men. My husband is outgoing and gregarious, George is reclusive and likes to keep things to himself. He can't help it, that's the way he is."

Erwin glanced back over his shoulder to make sure that Bland was safely out of earshot. "What does he do for a living?" he asked innocently.

"He owns several businesses including the prestige car showroom in the West End where Jeremy works."

"And your husband?"

"He's a financier, Mr Graham, he invests in ailing businesses and specialises in bringing them back to profit and then selling them. It has paid for everything you see around you in this house, but it's not been achieved without a great deal of hard work and the taking of substantial risks."

"I believe that's the same for most successful businesses," said Erwin solemnly. "Anyway, Mrs Seabourne, thank you very much again for inviting me in – I enjoyed our little conversation and I hope I have a chance to speak to you again soon. Would you mind if I call back sometime to see your husband and Jeremy?"

Minkie Seabourne gave the same gracious smile for Erwin's departure as she gave for his arrival.

"Please call back whenever you like," she said and they bade each other farewell.

He walked back down the drive to the place outside the gates where he had left his borrowed car, and when he got there he was surprised to see Mrs Brown the housekeeper waiting nearby.

"Hello," she said, "I guessed this was your car because there was nothing parked up by the house."

"That was a very nice cup of tea you made for us,"

Erwin said to her conversationally, wondering why she had taken the time and trouble to come down to the road and wait for him. "Apparently it was Earl Grey, though I'd never have known."

"Never mind about the cup of tea," she said in a quiet voice, "I heard you asking questions. Well there are a few things *I* can tell you, if you're interested to hear them."

"Yes, of course," he said. "Would you like to sit in the car?"

"Not now, there isn't time, I need to get back to the house before they notice I'm not there. But I've got half the day off from one o'clock. Can we meet somewhere? How about The Skipper's Inn? Will half-past one be all right for you? It'll be quiet in there at that time."

"The Skipper's Inn this afternoon at half-past one," repeated Erwin. "I'll be there."

Erwin's notes on Minkie Seabourne: An attractive and dominant woman who seems to relish the role of matriarch in a prosperous household and playing the perfect hostess. Can imagine her cracking the whip. Not sure what she really thinks of Rachel Summers. Treats her son Jeremy rather protectively, though maybe that is to be expected.
Impression – unsure of her sincerity.
Possible motive – nothing apparent.

Erwin's notes on George Bland: A colourless, insipid little man, but is this a front? He's watchful and suspicious. A long-time friend of the family and a regular house guest who seems to be involved in running several businesses, one of which employs Jeremy Seabourne.

Impression – unfavourable.

Possible motive – could be anything.

13

A Conversation At The Skipper's Inn

"Housekeepers see things that other people miss," said Rosanna Brown. "You don't have to go around looking, you just notice them. Small things." She sat on the window seat in the furthest corner of the lounge bar, fingering a glass of white wine. She had a pleasing, not unattractive face, a fulsome figure displayed beneath an outfit of casual clothes, for she had changed out of her housekeeper's apparel, and a pair of capable hands, the sort that Erwin thought could do anything. "I know Belle, we meet sometimes in the village shop and occasionally we come in here for a drink and a chat. Didn't know that, did you? She says you're an artist, so why were you pretending to be a newspaperman? That was a lie. Mrs Seabourne wouldn't like it if she knew she'd been lied to."

"Actually it wasn't," said Erwin Graham. "I used to work for a daily paper before I met her. Belle only knows me as an artist, and now I'm investigating a murder."

Rosanna Brown waved the matter aside. "It doesn't

make any difference to me what you are. When you came into the house and started asking her questions about Rachel, I couldn't help listening to what she was saying. Rachel was a lovely girl, I saw myself in her when I was that age. Free-spirited. She didn't know what she was getting herself mixed up in."

Erwin was sitting in a seat on the opposite side of the small round table, looking intently at the Seabournes' housekeeper. She took a drink from her glass. Her lips had bright red lipstick on them and they closed around the rim and he watched the pale liquid flow into her mouth. She put the glass down and ran her tongue over her lips, staring at him with big dark brown eyes. He stared back.

"You make it sound almost perilous," he said, taking a drink from his own glass of cider.

"It probably was."

"What exactly *did* you see?" he asked, "in your position as housekeeper?"

Rosanna's eyes narrowed shrewdly.

"I suppose it's no good asking if this information is worth anything to you?" she inquired hopefully.

"It's worth a great deal," he assured her, "but if you know Belle, as you say you do, you'll also know that we're as poor as church mice."

"I thought as much," she sighed.

"Never mind," said Erwin. "Why not settle for the glass of wine, and perhaps another?" And then he added, "We can't all be as well to do as the Seabournes, you know."

"That's the trouble," she said. "It gets you into the way of thinking that everyone's the same." She took another sip of wine. "Don't think I'm being disloyal to them for talking to you like this, I'm not. They've always been very good employers and treated me fairly. It's just that Mrs Seabourne told you things earlier that weren't strictly true."

Erwin smiled faintly.

"So she didn't mind lying to *me*."

Rosanna shrugged.

"They weren't necessarily lies – let's say they might have been misleading."

"In what way?"

"Her and Mr Seabourne have separate bedrooms. They've been like that for years. Well, Mr Seabourne – Charles, as he likes me to call him when Mrs Seabourne isn't around – has tried to get me into his room more than once since I've been there, but I'm having none of that sort of behaviour." She twiddled the wine glass around in circles on the table and cast Erwin a sidelong glance. "You can always tell when a bed has been slept in by more than one person, you know."

"Do you mean *Rachel?*" he asked incredulously.

She nodded.

"Yes, none other."

"They were having an affair?"

"I'd say they couldn't keep their hands off each other when they thought nobody was looking."

"When did this happen?"

"It went on for quite a long time. Rachel had known the family for years because she was a friend of Catherine's from childhood, and then she and Jeremy began having an attraction for each other and ended up getting engaged. She often used to stay at the house for the weekend – it probably began with one of their regular house-parties, I can't remember, to tell you the truth. Not that it matters. She always slept in Jeremy's bed when he was home, but then I started noticing that she would stay on even when he wasn't there. I live in myself, and it wasn't hard to tell that Rachel ended up in Charles's bed when Jeremy was absent. When I went into Charles's room in the morning to tidy up, I could tell that the bed had been used for having sex – there are always little tell-tale signs, you know."

"I can imagine. Did Mrs Seabourne know what was going on?"

"I would have thought so, if she's as observant as I am. On the other hand, if she had already cast her husband aside by insisting on separate bedrooms, there's not really a lot she could say. Anyway, you saw her with George, didn't you?"

"*Him?*"

"The west winds blow in a strange way in that house, I can assure you."

"Did Rachel's affair with Charles go on after she broke off her engagement to Jeremy?"

"As far as I'm aware, it was going on right up to the time of her death."

"So Jeremy could have had a reason to murder her if he found out, as could Charles if the relationship started going wrong, and even Minkie might have done it."

"It opens up all sorts of possibilities, doesn't it? A little word like blackmail comes to mind."

"Blackmail?"

"Think about it. She *could* have been blackmailing any one of them – even George. You know she had been pregnant, don't you?"

"I heard mention of a miscarriage," admitted Erwin. "I suppose it could have been *anybody's*."

"It certainly wouldn't have been Minkie's," said Rosanna flippantly. She picked her wine glass up again and drained it. "Ridiculous name for a woman of her age."

"I'll get you another," he muttered, took her empty glass and went over to the bar with it. The landlord of The Skipper's Inn was a jovial round-faced man in his fifties who spoke with a strong local accent.

"And what can I get you this time, Mr Graham, sir?" he asked, beaming hospitably at Erwin.

"Another glass of white wine for the lady, please," replied Erwin.

"The same as before," called out Rosanna from the corner. "Medium dry."

"Haven't seen you in 'ere for a little while now, Rosie," the landlord called back. He took a clean glass down from a rack above the bar and poured wine into it from a bottle.

"Tragic about Rachel," said Rosanna.

"Can't get over it, Rosie, just can't get over it. This place will never be the same again without her. Whoever could do such a wicked thing to a lovely young girl like Rachel? There you are, sir, one glass of wine. That'll be three pound fifty."

"Thank you." Erwin paid for it and carried it back to the table by the window. He put the glass down in front of Rosanna and resumed his seat. "When you talk about Rachel having affairs and raise the possibility of blackmail, it no longer sounds as if she's an innocent victim," he said.

"Rachel was a nice girl, and nothing can alter that fact," replied Rosanna, picking up her glass and raising it to her mouth with an appreciative smile, "so don't take it the wrong way. But I think she got out of her depth. What if the baby that she *might* have had was Charles's? What if it *had* been born? What if Charles had divorced Minkie and married Rachel himself? Or they may have simply chosen to live together. It raises all sorts of awkward possibilities, doesn't it? I think Rachel enjoyed life's little pleasures without realising for a moment that she was unwittingly putting herself in great danger."

"So do you think she was killed by a member of the household or one of her friends?"

"I believe the answer lies in West Winds."

"You realise that the police suspect Godfrey Sanderson, her new gentleman friend?"

"Is he the tall handsome man who came with her to the

house-party?" asked Rosanna, lifting her eyebrows in obvious disbelief. "The one I saw her going around with?"

"Yes."

"I'm sure it wasn't *him,*" she said in a tone of scepticism.

"Actually, Belle and I are both convinced he didn't do it, which explains why I'm investigating the case, but the police seem to think it *was* him. For my part, I managed to speak to Catherine Seabourne and Emma Richmond yesterday in Kingsbridge and, as you know, Minkie Seabourne this morning – together with George Bland, if you count that as a conversation. Later I intend going to Saltcombe to find James Carvell and his wife and their friend Robert Fairweather to see what they can tell me."

"Take my advice and speak to the Carvells separately," said Rosanna with a meaningful look.

"What will that achieve?" asked Erwin, sensing that the housekeeper was holding something back.

"James might be more forthcoming if you speak to him on his own."

"In what way?"

Rosanna rubbed her nose with one finger.

"Let's just say that I saw him and Rachel together once or twice at the house, usually in the middle of a party, and I don't think Julie would have approved if she had seen what I saw them doing. James is an old friend of Jeremy's, and Rachel would have known him long before he met Julie. It gets more interesting all the time, doesn't

148

it?"

"Two more suspects?" ventured Erwin.

"Depends how you look at it. Maybe the baby *wasn't* Charles's, perhaps James saw her as a threat to his marriage, or Julie found out and decided to do something about it herself. The possibilities are endless. If you keep digging, you'll probably find out a lot more – but I'm certain that the reason for Rachel's murder goes back to something that happened at West Winds."

"She didn't exactly lead an uncomplicated life," said Erwin, scratching his head. "All this business of living quietly on a farm, riding around on her horse and working down the pub in the evening – I'm getting the idea that Rachel had two completely different sides to her life."

"Isn't that true for many of us?" said Rosanna with a wry smile, studying her wine glass abstractedly, her mind deep in thought. "Anyway, I wish there was something I could do to help."

"There is."

She opened her big dark eyes questioningly and turned them to gaze across the table at Erwin.

"What's that?"

"Keep those beautiful eyes and ears of yours open all the more and let me know if you see or hear anything that seems in any way strange or suspicious. Also I want to speak to Charles and Jeremy when they show up. It would be very useful if you could tell me when they're back."

Rosanna seemed agreeable to the suggestion.

"Let me have your phone number and I'll call you if something happens," she said. "You were right about Jeremy – he'll be home by the weekend at the latest no matter what, otherwise young Emma will make his life an absolute misery. As for Charles, his business trips can last a week or more, but what's odd is that he always tells me beforehand so that I can get all his clean laundry together. He said nothing this time, I'm not even sure when he left, but it must have been late on Sunday, which is a bit unusual. At any rate, his Bentley wasn't parked on the drive the following morning."

"That was well after the time that Rachel's body was discovered," said Erwin thoughtfully.

"I'm not even sure when Jeremy left the house, either," mused Rosanna, shaking her head slowly. "There are so many unanswered questions."

"Indeed there are. Well, I'm driving over to Saltcombe this afternoon – would you like me to drop you off at West Winds on the way?"

"On my afternoon off?" retorted Rosanna in horror, and gave a laugh. "No thanks, I'm on my way to Kingsbridge to do a bit of shopping. The bus will be along in a few minutes."

They finished their drinks, left the pub and went their separate ways.

14

The Investigation Goes To Saltcombe

Saltcombe is one of life's pleasant watering places, still with more than a touch of faded Victorian gentility to it, a seaside town which occupies a prominent position on a rocky headland so that one part of it faces directly out over the English Channel whilst the other part, including the harbour, is sheltered within the mouth of the estuary, and small wooded coves add to a feeling of privacy and seclusion. It would have been the favoured destination of the wealthy classes in days gone by, and now it was a popular summer resort. It had an abundance of hotels and guest houses, many of Georgian architecture, a long attractive promenade with gift shops and restaurants, a lifeboat station and, hidden away in a tiny inlet behind the harbour, a small boat-builder's yard run by a man named Alfred Wallace, one of a dying breed of marine craftsmen. His yard was reached by travelling down a narrow lane and Erwin parked next to the main building, a large timber-clad shed. This is where Catherine Seabourne's information told him that he could expect to find Robert Fairweather, for he was Alfred Wallace's assistant. When not at work, he lived alone in a small fisherman's cottage at the end of a narrow winding lane near the harbour called Long Reach.

The fresh smell of the sea air met Erwin when he got out of the car, and he stood for a few moments admiring the view. In the foreground, a small slipway ran from the boat-builder's shed down to the water and, further out, his gaze took in a cluster of small boats moored well out in the middle of the river. They were mostly yachts and sailing dinghies, with a handful of small fishing boats amongst them. Larger commercial vessels were tied up inside the harbour, where charges would be more expensive. In the background he could hear the high-pitched whine of an electric power-tool being used.

Erwin could have spent the rest of the afternoon enjoying the view, because it made a wonderful scene for a painting, but he heard footsteps coming towards him from behind and turned to see an elderly white-haired man approaching. He was wearing a pair of well-worn brown corduroy trousers fastened around the waist by a large leather belt, an open-necked shirt and a jacket with patches on the elbows.

"Good afternoon, sir," he said amicably, "can I be of any help to you?"

"Would you be Mr Wallace, by any chance?" inquired Erwin.

The old gentleman stopped and bowed.

"None other than Alfred Wallace at your service, sir,"

he replied. "And I have pleasure in telling you that you have come to one of the finest boatyards on the south coast!"

"I thought as much," said Erwin. "There can't be many of you left."

"Very few indeed, sir, but we manage to keep ourselves going. What can I interest you in? A nice docile little skiff, maybe?"

Erwin shook his head solemnly.

"I used to get seasick on the Serpentine."

"Oh."

"Actually I was told that a certain Mr Fairweather works here, and I was hoping I might be able to have a word with him, if it's convenient."

"Do you mean Robert? Yes, he's inside, finishing off sanding down a hull."

That explained the whining sound of a high-speed hand-tool being used somewhere within the nearest building.

"He shouldn't be more than a couple of minutes and then I'll ask him to come out and see you," said Mr Wallace. "Or would you prefer to go inside?"

"I've never seen boats being made before," said Erwin with interest. "Do you think I *could* take a look inside?"

"Of course, dear sir! I'd be delighted to show you around. My grandfather started this business in 1881 and it's been in the family ever since. You can't imagine what it was like in its heyday. I think the 1920s and 1930s were the most exciting years in the firm's history. They were the days of unceasing pleasure for the well-to-do and we couldn't build enough boats to keep up with the demand. Never mind the Great Depression. They'd come down from London or their big country estates and they'd stay in the finest houses in the district and it was one long round of fun and enjoyment. Mind you, the sea around these parts can be treacherous when it wants to be, and there were a fair few tragedies with the young people full of high spirits and none too particular in their way of handling the craft. My father used to go on about it – he was young himself in those days, and more than once he had to go out to them when they got themselves into trouble and help them back to safer waters. Reckless young idiots with more money than sense, he used to say, and sometimes he was younger than they were! But of course he knew where all the dangerous currents were, and the submerged rocks. First went out to sea when he was four years old, so it was in his blood. And it's in mine, too. But not my own sons – they don't want to know! There's not the money in it now, you see, not for a small company like this one. They've got other ideas of how to earn a living, and boat-building doesn't come into it for them. Robert was my apprentice, and I suppose he'll keep it going after my days."

The sound of the sanding tool had stopped now and a young man appeared in the doorway of the workshop, brushing dust off himself. He removed his face-mask and coughed.

"Ah, Robert, there you are," said Alfred Wallace in a

kindly voice. "This gentleman has called to see you and he says he's interested in looking inside the shed, too, because he's never seen boats being made. You're just the one to show him, so can I leave you both together for a few minutes?"

Robert Fairweather nodded readily and beckoned Erwin over.

"Come this way," he invited. "What was it you wanted to see me about? Are you thinking of buying a boat?"

"No, I'm not here for that reason," said Erwin. "Actually I've come to have a word with you about Rachel Summers."

Robert Fairweather stopped and turned to him.

"Rachel?" he responded in surprise. "Then are you from the police?"

Erwin smiled and shook his head.

"No, nothing like that. I'm a crime reporter."

"Oh, the newspapers. I'm not sure if there's much I can tell you."

An upturned boat stood in the middle of the workshop floor and this was evidently what he had been working on. Erwin ran his fingers idly over the smooth surface of the hull and picked up a layer of fine dust on them. There was a pungent smell of resin in the enclosed atmosphere, although the windows were all open.

"It's reinforced plastic," said Robert in a tone of disgust, passing him a cloth to wipe his hand clean. "But that's mostly what people want these days. Produced from a mould, like jelly."

"You make it sound as if it's not to your liking."

"Timber is the only true material for boat-building," declared Robert Fairweather passionately, and Erwin began to see that what he had been told by Godfrey and Catherine in their accounts of the young man were perfectly true. "Even if you built two wooden boats to the same design, they would never be truly identical, there would always be a uniqueness to both of them. Boats made from a mould are – well, mass-produced!"

"I'm sure there must be advantages and disadvantages to each method," commented Erwin diplomatically.

Robert gave him what could only be described as a pitying look.

"Go on with what you were asking me," he said.

"How well did you know Rachel?"

He shrugged.

"Not particularly well, I wouldn't have said. I'm a friend of Jeremy Seabourne, and I saw her a few times when they were engaged and I've seen her a few times since they became disengaged."

"Did you like her?"

"Did I *like* her? Well yes, she seemed a nice enough girl. Very attractive and all that."

"You never went out with her?"

"What, me? Go out with her? Of course not, she was Jeremy's fiancée."

"But the engagement was broken off, as you said. I meant you never went out with her after that?"

"No, I just used to see her occasionally as one of the

156

gang of friends. Quite often we'd meet up and go to The Skipper's Inn in Watersford for a drink, and that's where she worked. It's called socialising."

Erwin nodded his head in understanding.

"Can you think why anyone would have wanted to kill her?" he ventured.

"I cannot think of any reason at all. It's a complete mystery to me – but as I said earlier, I didn't know her particularly well. Perhaps you ought to speak to somebody who was better acquainted with her."

"I was hoping to speak to Jeremy," admitted Erwin, "but he doesn't appear to be at home for the time being. You wouldn't know where he is, by any chance?"

Robert shrugged his shoulders.

"If he's not at home, I imagine he's in London."

"It should be easy enough to find out. Well, thank you, Mr Fairweather – I'm sorry I had to trouble you at work."

"Not at all. I'm sorry I couldn't be any more help, but there it is. I suppose we'll find out eventually what happened to Rachel. The police usually get to the bottom of these things."

"Don't let me keep you from your work," said Erwin with a smile, pointing at the partly-completed hull. "Purely out of interest, what sort of people buy this type of boat these days?"

"You'd be surprised," said Robert. "We have customers from all over the country – and not necessarily very rich people, either. Boating enthusiasts come in many different shapes and sizes, like the boats themselves."

"Mr Wallace was telling me that you're not as busy now as you were in days gone by."

"That's true, we're not. There used to be four of us working here when I first started, and more than that at one time. We do repairs as well, mind you, and that keeps us quite busy."

"But nothing much in wood these days?" said Erwin, tempting him back to his favourite subject.

"Sadly not. There are still boatyards that specialise in wood, but not this one. Anyway, if you'll excuse me, I'd better carry on here, unless there's anything else you have to ask."

"No, that's all I wanted to speak to you about. Thanks again."

Erwin Graham wandered casually back outside and found Alfred Wallace examining the keel of a boat in the yard, though he sensed that the old man was merely waiting for him to finish talking to his assistant.

"All done?" he asked.

"Yes, thank you. It's very interesting, what you do here."

"One of the oldest crafts, boat-building," said Mr Wallace contemplatively.

"You've got a reliable young assistant, by the look of it, to keep it going."

"Aye, Robert's a good lad."

"A shame he can't indulge his liking for wood more often," remarked Erwin with a smile.

"Ah yes, he's a great one for the old ways," said the

elderly gentleman, and began to look wistful. "But we get one or two in from time to time for repair, and he's happy enough then."

They exchanged a few more parting pleasantries and Erwin got into his car. He drove back down the narrow lane towards the harbour and then took a right turn which led him into Long Reach, where he noted that Robert Fairweather's address seemed to be the cottage at the far end of a terrace, with the upturned hull of a dinghy in the tiny front garden. "He lives conveniently near his workplace and the lifeboat station," mused Erwin quietly to himself. A few minutes later he was heading for Seaview House in Higher Lane which was the address he had been given by Catherine Seabourne for the Carvells. As the name of the road suggested, it was situated high above the town with a magnificent view across the English Channel. Erwin pulled up outside a large Victorian detached villa which had a big wooden sign hanging in the front garden proclaiming Seaview House Private Hotel. It was built of grey stone and had big sash windows and a certain flamboyance in the intricate carving of the barge boards above the front bay windows. The roof was topped by ornate ridge tiles. It looked solidly-built and comfortable.

Erwin Graham opened the wrought-iron gate and climbed up a steep flight of stone steps which led to the garden path. The front lawn was cut neatly short and a colourful variety of flowers adorned the borders. Someone obviously took a great deal of time and trouble looking after it.

He pressed the door-bell and heard a shrill ringing from within the house. Presently the front door was opened by a young woman who looked at him with the welcoming expression of a guest house landlady, but there was a hint of shyness behind the professional manner.

"Mrs Carvell?"

"Yes," she replied with an engaging smile.

"My name is Erwin Graham. I wonder if I could trouble you for a few minutes, please. I'm a journalist and I'm covering a story on the death of Rachel Summers."

"How interesting," she said, opening her eyes a little wider, and stepped back. "Would you care to come in?" She led the way into the front lounge. "Who were you hoping to speak to? Me or my husband?"

"Both of you, if possible."

"In that case you'll have to settle for me at the moment, my husband is rather busy in the kitchen getting things ready for the guests' evening meal." She smiled. "I run the part that you can see and do all the administrative work and leave him to do the cooking. It's a very good arrangement."

"It's certainly a lovely place," said Erwin, looking around the room in admiration.

"It belonged to James's parents and they ran it for many years but poor health forced them to retire, so James gave up his job and he and I took over the running of it. He grew up here – to him it's always been home as well as his family's business. Anyway, how can I be of help?"

"You knew Rachel, I understand."

"Only slightly. I used to see her at the Seabournes' house from time to time. I don't think it would be correct to say that I *knew* her but we were acquainted."

"Can you tell me anything about her?"

Julie Carvell considered.

"She was very pretty and I was envious of her good looks. Girls like her always seem to get everything, or so I thought. Funny how you can be envious of someone you don't really know, and now she's dead and all that prettiness is no longer."

"What did you think when you heard that she'd been murdered? Were you and your husband surprised?"

"*Surprised?* I don't think that's exactly the word I would use. Shocked and horrified would be more accurate."

"I used the word deliberately because sometimes people make enemies through things they have said or done. That doesn't excuse the murder, of course, but it might go some way towards explaining it."

"Oh, I see."

"Let me put it to you this way – someone decided to kill Rachel and there must have been a reason. Can you think what that reason might be?"

"Somehow I feel you're asking me to try and enlighten you on a matter I know nothing about. To me, she was no more than a girl I met a few times and had very little to do with."

"You and your husband went out on the boat trip with

161

her, didn't you, on the evening of the party? You sailed from Watersford to Saltcombe and back."

"Yes, that's right, we did."

"Can you remember who went altogether?"

Julie Carvell narrowed her eyes and frowned in thought.

"Hmmm," she said, "yes, I think I can remember. There weren't many of us. Starting with James and myself, we had Rachel, Jeremy, Catherine, Emma and Robert with us, and the older man whose name I forget, who came to the party with Rachel. Jeremy was at the helm and Robert went below to get the champagne."

"Oh, you had champagne on board?"

"Probably Jeremy's idea – he's rather extravagant and likes to show off a bit. Catherine was teasing him by calling him captain. He really should have been wearing a blazer and peaked sailor's cap!" She smiled to herself at a sudden recollection. "He had a glass of it in his hand and there was a bit of fooling around, drinking to everyone's good health, when we hit some rough water and he almost lost control. Robert wasn't very pleased because he nearly over-balanced and spilt his champagne!"

"Can you recall whose idea it was to go for the boat trip?"

"I think it was Jeremy's – after all, it *was* his family's boat. It was a nice warm evening and I suppose he thought it would be a good idea. Mind you, I got a bit cold on board. By the time we reached Saltcombe it was getting dark and chilly."

"Have you ever been out in the boat before?"

"Yes, James and I were invited out once before we were married. James, of course, has been out in it many times in the past because he's been a friend of Jeremy's for years. The only other time I've been out in it myself was when we went with Jeremy and Emma, just the four of us. Last year, it was. We put out to sea in it because he said we were going to do a trip over to France, and Emma was ever so scared. When the engine started playing up a bit, she became almost hysterical. He pretended it had sprung a leak, too. Then we hit some big waves several miles out, and the boat was pitching and rolling quite a bit and I started panicking as well, thinking we were going to sink, but he turned it around and we got back all right. We moored up off Saltcombe for the night." She giggled coyly. "It was rather romantic."

I daresay it was, Erwin thought to himself, wondering how Belle and he would manage in a small boat rocking about on the water.

"How well do you know Mr and Mrs Seabourne?" he asked, changing the subject.

"Charles and Minkie? I've only met them through James. They're lovely people and they seem to have absolutely *everything*. Some people are like that, though, aren't they?"

"And George Bland? Can you tell me anything about him?"

"That's the quiet little man who always seems to be visiting them, isn't it? No, I can't tell you anything about him at all, he keeps very much to himself and never says more than a few words – although sometimes he talks to James. I find him very distant and unfriendly. In fact, he gives me the creeps a bit. Whenever he's there, I always feel there's a bit of a strained atmosphere, if you know what I mean, although I don't know why. According to Minkie, he's got important business interests with Charles and they spend their time discussing deals and investments."

"How dreary," remarked Erwin, pulling a face. "Still, something has to be done to pay the bills."

"Have you seen the size of their house? It's a mansion, and must cost a fortune to run. It's such a big place, I don't think you would know what was going on at one end if you were at the other! No wonder they have a housekeeper."

"And how do you come to know them yourselves? You say you met them through James. What's the connection?"

"I'm an old friend of Jeremy's," said a new voice unexpectedly, and Erwin turned to see a young man standing in the open doorway. "Sorry, did I surprise you?"

"Oh, James, this gentleman is from the newspapers," said Julie. "Mr – Graham – wanted to ask us some questions about Rachel. He said he wanted to speak to both of us but I explained that you were busy in the kitchen."

"The potatoes are all done ready," said James Carvell, and advanced towards Erwin with an outstretched hand.

"How do you do, Mr Graham. In what way can we be of help?"

"Your wife has been telling me that you both knew Rachel Summers and that the last time you saw her was on Saturday at the Seabournes' house-party when a few of you went out in their boat."

"Oh, yes. Well what can I say? We simply can't believe such a dreadful thing could happen to poor Rachel. We were stunned by it. Tragic business." James Carvell was now standing in the middle of the room, staring warily at Erwin and glancing frequently at Julie. He knew he had come in on the conversation and was unsure of what had already been said. "Actually I met Rachel through knowing Jeremy. My parents have been friendly with the Seabournes for years – I think my father met Charles through the Royal Saltcombe Golf Club, where they were both members. As for going out on the *Sarah Jane* last weekend, well Jeremy's always been keen on sailing. He and I have known each other since we were very young. As boys we used to take the *Sarah Jane* down the river, usually without anyone knowing! My father had a boat, too, which he kept here in Saltcombe, down in the old family boathouse, but he was never taken with it as much as Charles was, and he sold it ages ago. Charles and Minkie would think nothing of sailing across the channel for the day. Sometimes they'd stop off in Guernsey or Jersey on their way back from visiting St Malo. Charles's friend George went with them a few times but he used to suffer from seasickness, apparently."

"Your wife was telling me that she finds him a very quiet little man."

"Yes, he is. I can't say I care for him very much. He's forever pestering us to sell him this place."

"Going back to Rachel, how did you get on with her?"

"I liked her," said James matter-of-factly. "Well, we both did, didn't we, Julie?"

Julie nodded in agreement.

"Yes, but you must have known her for quite a long time yourself, mustn't you?" said Erwin. "After all, wasn't she a friend of Catherine's to begin with?"

James seemed to hesitate.

"Oh, absolutely. Yes, that's quite right. I used to see her fairly often when we were younger."

"So when you say you liked her, it was more than merely a casual acquaintance? I mean, your wife would only count her in *that* respect, wouldn't she?"

James Carvell did not seem to know what to say. In the end he gave a nervous laugh and shrugged his shoulders.

"You know what it's like when you're a child – boys dislike girls and girls dislike boys. We never had much to do with each other at that time, but when you grow up, you regard people of your own age and the opposite sex differently."

Erwin nodded.

"Of course," he said. "Well, I don't think there's much else I can ask either of you. Thank you very much." He turned to smile at Julie Carvell, who smiled politely back. "I mustn't take any more of your valuable time, but I

166

would like to say how much I like this guest house of yours. What a superb view!"

"It is rather nice, isn't it?" said Julie proudly. "It's in one of the best positions to see out over the river *and* the sea."

"And it must take up so much of your time, both of you, running it."

"Oh yes, we're always very busy."

Erwin turned back to James Carvell.

"And your wife was telling me that you're in charge of all the cooking," he said. "You must be an expert chef!"

James smiled modestly.

"I wouldn't go as far as to say that. She probably told you that we took the place over from my parents a couple of years ago. Since then I've been learning how to do more and more ambitious things – some of these cooking programmes on television are very useful – though the breakfasts are always straightforward."

"Would you mind very much if I had a look in your kitchen, to see where it all goes on?"

"Not at all," said James, "I'd be delighted to show you. Follow me."

"And I have to make a few telephone calls," said Julie, "so would you excuse me, please, Mr Graham?"

Erwin followed James Carvell out of the lounge and down a long narrow hallway which led to the kitchen, where pots and pans were in various states of preparation for the evening meal.

"Now we're alone, I'll come straight to the point," said

167

Erwin, "because I didn't want to raise the matter in front of your wife. I'm given to understand that you and Rachel may have been having a bit of a fling, if that's the right way of putting it."

James Carvell reacted by turning around abruptly and staring in wide-eyed amazement.

"How the devil did you find that out?" he uttered in a hoarse voice.

"Is it true?"

Carvell drew a deep breath and lowered his gaze to the floor before replying:

"Yes, yes, it's true. Rachel and I got a bit carried away one night at the Seabournes' place. We'd had far too much to drink, and we just happened to bump into each other on the landing. I'd already had a bit of a disagreement earlier that evening with Julie over something fairly trivial and, well, before I knew what we were doing, Rachel and I were having a kiss and a cuddle, and next thing we were in one of the empty bedrooms. She was an exceptionally good lover, and she knew it. She also knew that she was far better than Julie could ever be – I know that's a terrible thing to say, but it was a fact!"

"How long did it go on, this fling?"

"We saw each other occasionally after that, but not very often."

"Where?"

"Where did we see each other? Different places. Sometimes we'd meet up in her car, sometimes my car. It was never here, or the farm. Once, believe it or not, we even paddled out in the little dinghy to the *Sarah Jane*, moored in the river below West Winds, and had a fantastic evening together. *That* was her idea." He gave a rueful smile. "Rachel had a wicked sense of humour. She'd finished with Jeremy by then, and felt she was getting one back on him."

"Correct me if I'm wrong, but your wife mentioned a romantic foursome when the pair of you went out for a sailing trip with Jeremy and Emma," said Erwin.

"It wasn't as good as when I was with Rachel," said James in a quiet voice. "I don't know why, but the bunk seemed a lot less comfortable with Julie, though she didn't complain. Rachel and I just seemed to float blissfully on the very same bunk, but it probably had more to do with Rachel's expertise. Look, I know it was wrong, but now poor Rachel's dead, don't expect me to regret it!"

"Did your wife ever find out about you and Rachel?"

An expression of horror came over James Carvell's face.

"Good Lord no! She's completely unaware of it. Please don't tell her, will you?"

"I have no intention of telling her," said Erwin, "but can you be certain she doesn't already know?" His eyes had been roving all around the kitchen and settled now on a row of sharp knives hanging on hooks. Carvell followed the direction of his gaze and the look of horror changed to one of revulsion.

"Surely you're not suggesting that – Julie – killed

169

Rachel? My wife would never be capable of doing such a thing!"

Erwin gave the faintest of smiles.

"I never imagined for one moment that she would be," he said. "After all, Mr Carvell, we're in the kitchen and this is *your* territory. Thanks for the little chat – I think you've told me all I needed to know. I can see myself out."

Erwin made his way back down the hall and let himself out of the front door. He felt that he was beginning to understand how all the pieces of the mystery fitted into place, but still there remained that elusive bit of information without which it was impossible to complete the picture.

It was time to leave Saltcombe and head back to Watersford.

Erwin's notes on Robert Fairweather: A hard-working, slightly intense young man. Rather peripheral to the group, and very much taken up with his job as a boat-builder. Seems quite open and honest.
Impression – favourable.
Possible motive – nothing obvious.

Erwin's notes on Julie Carvell: A pleasant enough young woman, not linked closely to Rachel other than through her husband, but does she know of his infidelity?
Impression – favourable.
Possible motive – jealousy.

Erwin's notes on James Carvell: A long-term friend of Jeremy's, so has close ties to the family and admits to an affair with Rachel. Somehow seems a bit cold towards the matter of her death.

Impression — note sure what to make of him.

Possible motive — fear of being blackmailed.

15

I Receive Another Visitor

"This is Superintendent Haworth," said Detective Sergeant Hoskins. Both men were standing on the doorstep of Hill Cottage, Hoskins giving me an affable smile of familiarity. His superior was a tall, broad-shouldered man dressed in a smart dark grey suit. He had the heavy angular features of a man who has played rugby football in his younger days and I noticed that he had very large hands, which had probably spent much of their time catching a ball. Now he was only intent on catching the wrongdoer, and those same large hands had probably felt many a collar.

"Good afternoon, Mr Sanderson," said the superintendent. "May I come in? My sergeant here has already spoken to you on two previous occasions, but I would like to ask you some questions myself."

We went into the living room and I invited them to sit down. Superintendent Howarth seated himself carefully in the chair that Hoskins had previously occupied, leaving the sergeant to find a smaller seat by the fireside. I sat in my usual place. Haworth got straight to the point.

"I want to hear in your own words, Mr Sanderson, about the relationship you had with Miss Summers. I know what you said to Sergeant Hoskins when he spoke to you on the first occasion of seeing you, but it is important for me to hear the precise details, if you don't mind."

"Am I under suspicion?" I asked bluntly, unable to stop the question from coming out.

"At the moment you are our most important witness, and I want you to understand that you are being questioned as a witness and not as a suspect. *At the moment*." He repeated with emphasis.

"But you've taken my car away for examination," I pointed out.

"Yours is the only vehicle that we can presently link to Miss Summers's last known movements, and therefore we have no choice but to subject it to a thorough scientific examination, if only to eliminate it from the inquiry," explained the superintendent. "In a murder investigation, this is how things are done, and we cannot be too particular about offending people's sensibilities. If you would care to notice, Mr Sanderson," he went on, "I have taken the decision to call on *you* today, and not ask one of my officers to bring you to the police station. I wish to have a detailed understanding of the locality and not just the scene of the crime."

I sat back in my chair. "You asked me to tell you about the relationship I had with Rachel," I said, and gazed up

173

at the ceiling. "Very well. Put yourself in the position of someone who has recently come to live in a new place and finds that one of the first people he speaks to is a beautiful young woman who happens to be riding her horse along the river. It's one of the unlikeliest encounters you could ever imagine. She immediately makes him feel welcome to his new surroundings and invites him down to the pub in the village where she works in the evening. There, she introduces him to some friends of hers and the next thing he knows, he's been invited to a party at the home of one of these friends. Effectively, he is being swept along by events. At the party, they go for a delightful evening trip in a pleasure boat down the river as far as Saltcombe, and the atmosphere is one of ever-increasing romance. After the party, he takes her home and she gets out of his car and they part with a simple goodnight kiss. That is the last he sees of her." I brought my gaze back down to the superintendent. "*That* is the essence of the relationship. Older man meets younger woman and falls in love for the second time in his life."

Haworth nodded his head slowly.

"Did Miss Summers ever talk about anyone else in the short time you knew her?"

"She never mentioned anybody at all. She would hardly be likely to tell me about all her previous boyfriends, would she? And I would hardly be likely to ask. It's one of those things you *don't* talk about. I imagine a good-looking and vivacious girl like her would have had plenty of admirers in the past."

"I can assure you, Mr Sanderson, that we are following several lines of inquiry in that respect. At the present moment, there seems to be no obvious motive. Tell me, on that last time you saw her alive, did she say anything to explain how or why she came to be found on the tidal road?"

"No. The only thing she said to me was that she would have to see to her horse in the stable before going to bed. I assume she went straight there after getting out of the car."

Superintendent Haworth scratched his head.

"There's nothing to indicate whether she went to the stable or not, unfortunately. If the only purpose of going there was to check that her horse was safely settled down for the night that would not, in itself, leave any visible sign of having been accomplished. So she may, or may not, have visited the stable. And even if she did, it doesn't provide us with an explanation as to why she ended up on the tidal road. The only conclusion I can come to is that when she arrived at the stable, somebody was there waiting for her."

The same thought had already crossed my mind.

"We already know that the tide was in that night," continued the superintendent, "and you had to drive back the long way in order to get from West Winds to Watersford, so theoretically somebody else from the party could have got there first. But that would have meant going through deep water – and for what purpose?

Did somebody set out with the intention of killing her, or did it come about as the result of an argument?"

"Do you think it *does* involve one of the people at the party?" I asked him, hoping that his reasoning was drawing him away from suspecting me.

He shrugged.

"It seems very unlikely that one of her friends from the past would just happen to think of lying in wait for her at the stable at around midnight without any certainty of her being there – it's stretching things too far. If they knew nothing about the party, it would suggest that they were lying in wait for her every night for a period of time, and if that were the case I would expect them to be there earlier to coincide with her return from working in the pub. We cannot discount the possibility that the murderer could be one of the farmhands. But if we rule out a casual friend or acquaintance, that brings us back to the people at the party. Unfortunately," he went on, staring straight at me, "there is no evidence to support your own account of taking her home after the party. The evidence obtained so far tells us that you both left West Winds together in your car, but after that, there are no confirmed sightings of the car anywhere along the route. You can see my problem, can't you?"

Indeed I could. In spite of the friendly tone of his voice, and reasonable assertions to the contrary, Superintendent Haworth regarded me as his one and only suspect. I could give him my side of the story as much as I liked but there was nothing to *prove* that I hadn't murdered Rachel any more than he had reasonable cause to believe that somebody else *had* done it. I began to think that he was playing a game with me, trying the psychological approach to see if I might give myself away or break down and confess. I could appreciate that in his view, the chances of Rachel Summers going from being alive at her home one minute to ending up dead in the mud beside the tidal road the next by some unknown hand were far less likely than a good old lovers' argument that went wrong. The man sitting in front of me, looking directly and unflinchingly into my eyes, might well be a high-ranking detective, but he still, in all likelihood, worked on the balance of probability, and I could sit there myself, returning his scrutiny as innocently as I might, but his thoughts would still come to the same conclusion: guilty.

Perhaps I hadn't helped the matter when I said to him earlier that the essence of my relationship with Rachel was older man meets younger woman and falls in love for the second time in his life.

I could imagine, to my horror, his train of thought:

"Do I take that to understand you had fallen very much in love with this young lady?" "Why, yes, Superintendent, I would say that's perfectly true – I *had* fallen very much in love with her." "And this was the second love affair of your life?" "Well yes, I would count my wife as my first experience of love." "So this relationship meant a great deal to you?" "Oh absolutely, I was besotted with her." "But did the lady return your affection with the same degree of ardour and passion, Mr Sanderson, or did she refuse to acknowledge your feelings for her and is *that* why you killed her, Mr Sanderson, in a fit of uncontrolled anger, knowing that she didn't want you?"

My dilemma seemed to be getting worse.

16

I Taste Belle's Cooking

"I'm pleased to see you're still a free man," said Erwin when I arrived at his place just before seven o'clock.

"Only by a short margin, I fear," I replied in trepidation. "I had a visit from Superintendent Haworth today and I'm certain he's convinced that I did it."

"Without evidence he cannot charge you, no matter what he thinks, and if you didn't do it, how can there be any evidence?" Erwin's logic seemed impeccable. "Come in and sit down at the table. Belle's been busy in the kitchen all afternoon and I think dinner is nearly ready."

He led me into his small back room where the table had been neatly laid and I sat in one of the dining chairs. Belle called out a greeting from the kitchen and I raised my voice to reply:

"Good evening, Belle!"

A few moments later she entered the room carrying a tray containing three steaming bowls of soup and set them down on the table. Erwin was uncorking a bottle of wine.

"By way of a little celebration," he explained. "I'm making progress with my inquiries and you haven't yet been arrested, so I think that provides us with a good excuse for a glass of wine."

He poured some wine into three glasses.

"Good health!" he proposed, and we all touched our glasses together and had a drink. After that, we got on with the soup, which was apparently one of Belle's own special recipes made from vegetables grown in their small back garden. She assured me that it was the staple diet of the travelling gipsy. Whatever its origin, it tasted very good. She had baked small bread rolls to eat with it. "What is particularly interesting," said Erwin, getting back to the subject of the investigation in between spoonfuls of soup, "is that I have adopted the role of a newspaper reporter in all of my conversations so far, and you might expect the people I'm approaching to object to the intrusiveness of the press – indeed, Catherine Seabourne made her feelings quite obvious in that respect. Everybody else has received me quite matter-of-factly, but I was rather hoping that my presence, and questions, *would* make them react with anger because it would be perfectly natural for them to do so. By my reckoning, only the guilty person would make a point of staying calm and polite!"

"So their reactions give you no clues?" I asked.

"None at all."

Erwin then began his account of the day's proceedings, and there was so much to tell me that he was still describing his morning's visit to West Winds when we finished the soup and Belle disappeared back into the kitchen to fetch the next course, which was rabbit pie with potatoes, peas, runner beans, carrots and gravy, most of which seem to have been obtained from within a small radius of the house and not necessarily with the owner's permission.

"Belle has the ability to produce the most wonderful meal from very limited resources," Erwin informed me proudly between mouthfuls. "It's her upbringing, of course. I would have no idea how to eat off the land myself." With the main course under way, he moved on from West Winds to tell me about his conversation with Rosanna Brown during their lunchtime drink in The Skipper's Inn. The Seabournes' housekeeper seemed to provide the first tangible clues to possible motive.

"Miss Summers seems to have had a lively approach to life," commented Erwin drily, and gave me a pat on the shoulder. "Probably too lively for you, my friend," he said in a consoling tone. "I think we're beginning to get a better understanding of what might have brought about her murder, although at this stage I cannot tell whether it was jealousy, blackmail or fear."

"I can follow your line of thinking that it could have been jealousy or blackmail," I conceded. "If she were having several relationships at once, I should say that jealousy is a distinct possibility. And if she had been expecting a baby, perhaps she was blackmailing the father, especially if it *did* happen to be Charles Seabourne

– you know what I mean, "If you don't give me such-and-such at once, I'll tell your wife", that sort of thing. But fear? Fear of what?"

"From the things that Rosanna Brown told me," said Erwin, "Mr and Mrs Seabourne have been sleeping in separate bedrooms for a number of years so we can assume that they had drifted apart from one another as far as sexual relations are concerned. So Mr Seabourne – Charles – starts having a passionate affair with Rachel behind Jeremy's back and the next thing they discover is that she's pregnant. If Mrs Seabourne – Minkie – learns of the affair and sees with her own eyes that Rachel is expecting a baby, she might put two and two together and conclude that Charles could end up asking her for a divorce, or simply leave her for Rachel, and that makes her own position suddenly very insecure. Perhaps she fears that Charles and Rachel will start a new life together and cut the rest of the family out of his will. After the miscarriage, Minkie would have breathed again – there was at least a temporary reprieve – but it wasn't necessarily going to last forever. If Charles and Rachel were continuing with their affair, it might only be a matter of time before Rachel became pregnant again, particularly if that's what they wanted to happen. Minkie may have seen Rachel as a continuing threat and decided to do away with her."

"Is that what you think?" I asked incredulously. "Do you seriously believe that Minkie is the murderer?"

"I think it's a distinct possibility which puts her high up

the list of suspects," said Erwin, and turned to Belle. "What's your opinion?"

"If I were in that position, I would think very seriously about murdering her," said Belle with an emphatic nod of the head.

"You might *think* it, but would you actually go as far as to *do* it?" I retorted.

"Ah, now I didn't say I could put myself into Mrs Seabourne's *mind*," added Belle. "To do that, I'd have to know more about the sort of woman she is and what's at stake."

"The whole of the family fortune, perhaps," surmised Erwin thoughtfully. "After all, we don't know how it's tied up, or how much Minkie is entitled to in her own right. Theoretically, she could be left with very little if Charles has total control of their assets and was vindictive enough to cut her out. In other words, the motive is money."

"But wait a minute," I protested, "this doesn't exactly fit in with everything we've been hearing about how close the family was, and how upset they all were when they heard of Rachel's death."

"That might just have been a public show of unity," said Erwin, "whilst they each assessed the situation from their own point of view. Don't forget we've also been told how upset Charles was when he heard of Rachel's death. Well, of course, he *would* be, wouldn't he, if they were secret lovers? And if Minkie really hated or feared Rachel enough to murder her, she's hardly going to turn around afterwards and say so, is she? Instead, she'll bend over backwards to tell everyone how wonderful she thought Rachel was."

"If Rosanna's story is true," said Belle, "that Charles and Minkie *were* living separate lives under the same roof and that Charles *was* having an affair with Rachel which had resulted in a pregnancy, then Minkie *must* be lying by making out how sad she was about Rachel's death, whether she's guilty or not."

"And where does George Bland fit into all this?" I asked.

"Rosanna implied that Bland has something going with Minkie," replied Erwin. "In her words, 'the west winds blow in a strange way in that house'. She also said another thing that I found very interesting. She said that Charles had gone off on one of his business trips without telling her, which was unusual because she sorts out his laundry. He must have gone on the Sunday evening, which is only a few hours after hearing the news about Rachel and apparently taking it quite badly. To me, there's something odd about that which doesn't add up. His mistress found brutally murdered in the morning...a long business trip in the evening...goes off without telling the housekeeper as he usually does." Erwin sat back and pursed his lips, as if that was all he had to say, but then a sly look crossed his face. "However, let us not be too hasty in rushing to judgment. Rosanna had another little bit of information that needs to be weighed carefully – it seems that Rachel was also having an affair with James

Carvell!"

By now we had finished our main course and the plates were cleared away to make room for the dessert, which Belle proudly carried into the room in a big crystal glass bowl. It was a strawberry soufflé topped with fresh whipped cream and looked delightfully mouth-watering. She served it into three small dishes and we savoured each spoonful slowly. The conversation ceased whilst we did so. When the last bit of it was eaten, Erwin poured out more wine and we settled back to hear the final part of his day's work, visiting Robert Fairweather and the Carvells in Saltcombe. There was little information to arouse much interest in Robert's account, but when Erwin told us about his visit to Seaview House and his conversation firstly with Julie and then with James Carvell, we listened in complete silence.

"Any one of them could have done it," I said at last when he had finished telling us. "Apart from Robert Fairweather, there's not a single one of them who *didn't* have a reason to murder Rachel!"

"Quite so. The only one I think we can safely exclude from the list of household members and their friends is Rosanna Brown, she seems to be no more than a spectator to what's been going on, and a very useful source of information. And I can't think of a plausible reason why Robert Fairweather would have wanted to kill Rachel, either, unless he resented her making fun of him over his rather intense obsession with wooden boat construction – but I suppose there have been stranger

185

motives than that."

"So where do we go from here?" I asked.

"There are two people I have yet to speak to – Charles and Jeremy – and neither of them can be got hold of. Jeremy is expected back before next weekend, but Charles seems to have vanished in more mysterious circumstances, and he's the one who particularly worries me because I feel that his is the key role in trying to unravel what exactly Rachel got herself mixed up in. I certainly don't think she was attacked at random, I believe there was a definite reason. Unfortunately, her attractiveness to men has somewhat complicated matters and we've ended up with a large number of suspects. However, for the purpose of this investigation I think we should concentrate our attention on Charles Seabourne and find out where he is."

"Could you go back one moment to what Julie Carvell said about West Winds," I requested, "because I'm sure she said something that could be of great significance."

"She described it as a mansion," said Erwin, looking at his notes of the conversation, "and said it was such a big place that you wouldn't know what was going on at one end if you were at the other."

"It's certainly a very large house," I agreed, thinking back to my visit, "and part of it seems to form a separate wing at the rear."

"I can tell you more about that bit," said Belle suddenly. "Rosanna described it to me once, when we were talking together down at The Skipper's Inn."

"I didn't even know you were acquainted with her until she told me," grumbled Erwin.

Belle poked her tongue out at him. "There are *lots* of things you don't know about me!" she said playfully. "May I carry on with my story? She said Charles has his study there, in a sort of annexe, and there are several other rooms that are usually empty, unless they have a houseful of people when they become guest rooms. At one time they used to have really big weekend parties, but nowadays they're usually smaller so the rooms hardly ever get used. Rosanna said it made her life a lot easier."

"So it's possible that Charles *could* still be at West Winds without anyone knowing," said Erwin slowly. "*That's* an interesting thought."

"And there's one other thing you might like to know," added Belle. "Charles owns a gun, which he keeps locked in a drawer of his desk in the study. His father was an officer in the army during the last war, and gave it to Charles a few years ago shortly before his death. It's just an ordinary standard issue service revolver, but apparently it saved his father's life during the fighting in France after D-Day, so it's more than just a souvenir. Charles keeps very quiet about it because he hasn't got a gun licence."

"If that's the case, how does his housekeeper know about it?" I asked.

"She knows a lot of the family's secrets, and she told me that he showed it to her one day when he was trying to seduce her. She said she was very unimpressed by it, but apparently he keeps it with a small box of ammunition, so presumably it still works."

"I wonder if Rachel knew about it," mused Erwin.

"Depends. Perhaps he showed it to all of his prospective ladyfriends. 'Come over here and see what I've got' – that kind of thing."

"But anyway it doesn't provide us with any further clues to Rachel's murder. She was stabbed, not shot. If he owned a collection of daggers, that might be more relevant."

"You seem to have discovered some very interesting facts about the Seabourne family," I said, "but it certainly doesn't appear to get us any nearer to understanding why Rachel died. It points to several possible motives, but it's all supposition. What are you proposing to do next?"

"We need to find out when Charles is coming back – if he ever went anywhere in the first place," said Erwin. "Belle and I have already come up with an idea of how we might be able to do that. Belle, would you mind?"

Belle quietly got up from the table with a knowing little smile and went out of the room. This was evidently something they had been planning between themselves.

"I believe that Charles holds the key to this mystery," continued Erwin, "and the fact that he has gone away so soon afterwards, supposedly on a business trip, may be perfectly genuine, but the timing of it, and the decidedly out-of-character circumstances – leaving without telling his housekeeper – makes me wonder if it is connected with the murder in some way. Why go so late on Sunday evening? Surely it would be far more likely that he would make an early morning start on Monday?"

"Perhaps he had a long way to travel," I suggested, trying to think of a good reason.

Erwin didn't seem too persuaded by the idea.

"Possibly," he replied in a doubtful voice.

"What about his car? If he's gone away – for whatever purpose – his car won't be there, will it? If he's hidden himself away inside the house, he will also have to conceal his car."

"We need some answers," agreed Erwin, "but both you and I are now known at West Winds, so there will have to be another way of getting them. Belle!"

"I'm ready," called back Belle from the other side of the living room door.

"Come in and show Godfrey," said Erwin, and the door opened. In came Belle, dressed in her best gipsy costume – yellow cotton smock with frills, a long flowing red skirt and black boots. Her wavy raven black hair hung loosely below her shoulders and she wore a pair of large gold ear-rings. In one hand she carried a small wickerwork basket and I noticed that she had placed a variety of ornate rings on her fingers.

Erwin clapped his hands in delight at the sight of her.

"This is the Belle I discovered one day by the roadside," he explained, "and it's how she's going to call at West Winds."

"Selling my wares and telling fortunes," she added.

I stared at them both in amazement and suddenly we all

189

burst out laughing.

"But then comes the best bit," said Erwin.

"I claim to be having an affair with Charles and demand to see him!"

"And when is this little charade going to take place?" I inquired.

"This evening," replied Erwin.

17

Where Is Charles Seabourne?

We set off from Erwin's little tin shack at half-past eight in the borrowed car. He sat at the wheel with Belle alongside and I went in the back. The river was quite low, the tide now well out, so the road between Watersford and West Winds was almost dry between the long lines of marker posts and we covered the short distance in no time, stopping in a small lay-by partly hidden by trees further up the hill from the entrance to West Winds.

Erwin turned to Belle.

"You know what to say?" he asked, and she nodded.

"I met Charles at the county fair two weeks ago and we fell madly in love with each other. We went back to my caravan and he told me we should run away together. He promised to marry me if my family didn't mind and said he wanted lots of children," recited Belle with a big grin.

"Do you think they'll believe it?" I said.

She turned to give me a sidelong glance and pulled her frilly smock down to expose more bosom. "They'll believe it," she assured me.

"We need to find out about his car, too, so don't forget to mention it to Rosanna," said Erwin and leaned across to give her a kiss. "Be careful."

She gave him a superior look.

"This," she said, "is what I do best of all." And with that remark, she got out of the car and disappeared silently along the road.

"Do you think she'll be all right?" I asked anxiously, and Erwin, after a few moments' hesitation, gave a slow nod.

"She knows how to look after herself," he replied, "and Rosanna Brown's there, too, so that should ensure that nothing untoward happens. All we can do is sit here and wait. I wish we could have gone up there with her, to look for Charles's white Bentley, but it would be too risky."

Whilst we remained in the car, parked a short distance from West Winds, Belle walked quickly to the big gates of the house and turned in, making her way up the drive. Against the landscape of tall trees and hedges, she looked a somewhat incongruous figure, dressed in her brightly-coloured clothes, with an air of flamboyance and exotica about her. Although it was still daylight, the shadows of evening were increasingly darkening the approach to the house and some of the windows were already showing lights from within the building. Remembering what Erwin had said about Charles's car, she peered at several vehicles parked at the top of the driveway. They all looked new and could have belonged to anybody. She walked up to the front door and boldly rang the bell.

She breathed a sigh of relief when Rosanna Brown opened it, and the housekeeper gaped at Belle as if she could not believe what her eyes were seeing.

"Belle?" she said at last. "Is it you? What on earth are you doing, dressed up like that?"

Belle put her finger to her lips, and the last of Rosanna's words came out merely as a hoarse whisper.

"Erwin needs to know a few more things, and we decided that the best way to find out was for me to come here like this," she replied in a low voice. "I want to ask Mrs Seabourne when her husband will be back, but she won't just tell me the answer if she doesn't want to, so we thought of a way that might do the trick."

"Is this all part of it?" asked Rosanna in perplexed amazement, indicating to the costume.

"Yes! So as not to arouse anybody's suspicions, pretend I'm a passing gipsy. Invite me in."

"*What?* I'd lose my job if I let you into the house looking like that!"

"No you won't. I've got a particular reason to speak to Mrs Seabourne. She won't refuse to see me when she knows what it's about. Who's in the house altogether?"

"Mrs Seabourne's in the lounge, Catherine's upstairs in her room and George Bland is somewhere around. There's nobody else here, apart from myself."

"What about Jeremy?"

"He's not at home."

"And Mr Seabourne?"

"He's not here either."

"Are you quite sure?"

"Of course I'm quite sure!"

"Who do the cars outside belong to?" Belle pointed to the three vehicles standing on the drive, but before Rosanna could answer, a door opened across the hallway and Mrs Seabourne's voice called out:

"Who is it, Mrs Brown?"

Rosanna lowered her voice. "Not now – keep it till later," she said in a whisper, then stepped backwards from the door to turn around and call in reply: "It's someone who says she wants to see you, Mrs Seabourne."

"Say I've got something to tell her!" hissed Belle.

"She says she's got something to tell you."

Footsteps approached quickly across the hall and Minkie Seabourne came up and stood beside her housekeeper.

"Yes?" she said in an imperious voice. "Can I help you?" When she saw a colourfully-dressed gipsy girl standing on the doorstep, her expression changed to one of outright hostility. Gipsies had been known to call at the house before, and she usually sent them away with a stern warning. This one looked particularly bold and buxom.

"Are you Mrs Seabourne?" asked Belle.

"Who are you?" came the peremptory reply.

"I'm Belle. I want to see Charles, but this woman says he's not at home."

"I'm sorry but I really don't understand," said Minkie,

trying to remain polite. "Why should you want to see my husband?"

"Well, it's a bit difficult to explain, standing out here. Can I come in?"

Something began to dawn in the mind of Minkie Seabourne, something that she did not like, and she knew that she had no alternative but to let the woman into her house. She stood back and continued to cast a cold gaze at Belle.

"This way," she said curtly. "Thank you, Mrs Brown."

Belle entered the hall and followed Mrs Seabourne's tall statuesque figure across the parquet floor to the lounge. Once inside the room, Minkie closed the door and turned sharply to her visitor.

"Now then, kindly explain what this is all about."

"I've fallen in love with Charles," blurted out Belle, putting on her best act. "We met at the county fair and he says he wants to spend the rest of his life with me and have lots of children!"

Minkie stared at her for a few moments and finally gave a snort of derisive laughter.

"How preposterous!" she answered in a withering voice. "My husband – fall in love with *you?* You're out of your mind!"

"What's wrong with that?" demanded Belle hotly. "I'm a perfectly respectable woman! Anyway," she added in a huff, "he told me he'd never met anyone so beautiful in his entire life." I hope I'm not overdoing it, she thought to herself, pleased with her performance so far.

Minkie paused to study her more carefully. There was no denying that she was a very attractive young woman, with a pair of the most alluring eyes she had ever seen, and she could well imagine her husband falling for this luscious, sensuous creature. Charles had great difficulty controlling himself with women, as his wife was only too well aware. So what did the girl want, coming to the house like this?

"I don't know what you hope to achieve by walking in here and speaking to me in this brazen manner," said Minkie Seabourne, "but you cannot see my husband."

"But I *must* see him!" said Belle, raising her voice and stamping her foot on the floor.

"You cannot see my husband because he's not here!"

"He *is* here! You're just trying to prevent me from seeing him. I know you are!" Belle's eyes were blazing and her voice kept rising higher.

"Young woman," said Minkie Seabourne in a voice that sounded dangerously threatening, "if you do not leave this house immediately, I am going to call the police."

The door opened and George Bland came into the room.

"I thought I heard voices," he said in his cool detached manner. "Oh! I see we have a visitor." At the sight of Belle, his usually unflappable demeanour slipped by a notch or two and a look of fear and uncertainty came over him for an instant before he regained control.

"Another of Charles's fancy women," said Minkie in disgust. "She's come here saying she wants to see Charles,

196

but even though I've told her he's not here, she won't listen so I've said I'm going to call the police."

Bland interceded immediately in a calming voice.

"There's surely no need to do that," he said soothingly. "Young lady, would you allow me to say a few words to you? Charles is not at home at the present time and is unlikely to be here for several more days. He's away on business, so you see there's absolutely no point in waiting. We'll tell him about your visit as soon as he gets back – that's all we can do." He finished with a deprecating smile.

"When *is* he coming back?" demanded Belle, determined not to be put off by a vague answer.

Bland made an expansive gesture with his hands.

"Alas, I cannot say."

Belle turned to Minkie.

"*You* must know if you're his wife."

"Charles rarely discusses his comings and goings with me and in view of his many extra-marital affairs that is hardly surprising. I no longer care what he's doing, and it's more than likely that he's in the company of some woman at this very moment."

Belle took a deep breath and her bosom rose up magnificently inside her smock.

"*I don't believe you!*" she shouted, and ran out of the room into the hall. "I know he's here somewhere, and I'm going to find him!"

Minkie Seabourne and George Bland exchanged horrified glances.

"She's gone mad, what shall we do?" said Minkie desperately.

"Go after her!" came Bland's terse reply. "And if necessary, show her that the house *is* empty! When she sees he's not here, perhaps she'll leave us alone!"

Minkie Seabourne ran out into the hall, where she saw Rosanna trying to calm Belle down without realising that it was all pretence. Her housekeeper turned to her despairingly as if she didn't know what to do.

"All right, Mrs Brown," said Minkie in an authoritative voice, "the young lady is obviously very worked up and distraught. Would you kindly show her around the house to prove to her that Mr Seabourne is *not* here at the present moment." And with that, she turned on her heel and went down the hall to get as far away as possible from the dreadful intruder. George Bland went back into the lounge and closed the door.

Belle looked at Rosanna in expectation of a guided tour, but once Mrs Seabourne was out of sight she could no longer suppress her laughter.

"Well, you heard what the lady of the house said, show me around," she giggled.

Rosanna shook her head in disbelief.

"Whose idea *was* this?" she asked.

"Erwin said you told him you were puzzled that Charles had gone off late on Sunday night without making any of his usual arrangements," said Belle. "He thinks that Charles might actually still be in the house somewhere."

"But why?" asked Rosanna. "What would be the point of that?"

"He doesn't know – he just senses that Charles and Rachel were planning to set up a new life together, and that's what might have caused her death."

"You mean that whoever killed her wants to kill him too?"

"Yes. He thinks that Mrs Seabourne has something to do with it."

"Well if Charles was trying to hide from *her*, she *wouldn't* know he's still here, would she?"

Belle shrugged. The matter seemed to defy all logic.

"We simply thought this would be a good way of trying to find out," she said. "That's why I was asking you about the cars parked outside on the drive – who do they belong to?"

Rosanna gave a sigh.

"That's not going to help you very much – Catherine's is the sporty little Ford, Minkie's is the Mercedes and Jeremy's is the Jaguar. Charles usually parks his Bentley next to Minkie's Mercedes, he doesn't bother to put it in the garage around the back."

"Oh."

"Come on, I'd better show you around the house," said Rosanna, and deliberately raised her voice. "When you've seen all the rooms, young lady, Mrs Seabourne would like you to leave."

They commenced their search of the house, with Belle still playing the part of the lovelorn gipsy girl looking for her middle-aged paramour. Rosanna conducted her to every room, and Belle made a careful note in her head about each one. When they came to Catherine's bedroom, Rosanna knocked softly on the door because she expected the room to be occupied, but there was no answer.

"She must have gone out somewhere," muttered the housekeeper, and quietly opened the door to look inside. The room was empty. When they had completed their inspection of all the upstairs rooms in the main part of the house, they turned their attention to the annexe, where Charles had his study, and in which there was a further suite of bedrooms, but each one was unoccupied. The whole house was pervaded by an unnatural silence, with not a sound to be heard anywhere other than their own footsteps and the occasional ticking of a clock. They hardly spoke a word to each other in order to avoid disturbing the peace and quiet, and Belle felt a sense of foreboding in the surreal atmosphere of emptiness that seemed to have settled throughout the building.

It was when the two women were making their way back down the main staircase into the hall that they heard a muffled bang followed by a sharp cry of exclamation and a dull thud. Belle stopped halfway down the stairs and threw an uneasy glance at Rosanna.

"What was that?" she said in a half-whisper.

"I don't know," replied Rosanna hesitantly. "It came from over there." She pointed to the door of the lounge. There was no further sound to be heard from inside the house, except for the heavy ticking of a grandfather clock in the hall, but they both had the distinct impression of hearing running footsteps that appeared to come from outside – footsteps running on gravel.

Belle was suddenly seized by a feeling of panic, as if something dreadful had taken place, and she ran down the last of the stairs and crossed the hall to the lounge door. She grasped the handle and flung the door open.

Everything looked the same as it had done a few minutes earlier, when she had stood in the middle of the room talking to Mrs Seabourne, and George Bland was still in there, but there was one difference. He now lay on the floor, sprawled on the Persian rug in front of the fireplace, and there was a small hole in the centre of his forehead from which blood was trickling and forming a grotesque red pool beside him. George Bland was dead. And at the opposite end of the room, the French windows were ajar and the cool evening breeze was gently blowing the curtains.

18

The Gunshot Resounds

"Now let's get this straight," said Superintendent Haworth slowly, looking squarely at Belle. "You were here to ask the whereabouts of Mr Charles Seabourne, and you, Mr Graham and Mr Sanderson," he turned in our direction, "were waiting for her in a car parked up the road."

"That's exactly what happened, Superintendent," answered Erwin patiently.

"And all because Miss Belle here claims she was having an affair with Mr Seabourne." Haworth rubbed his chin thoughtfully. "Except that she wasn't really having an affair with him at all, she was just pretending."

"As a means of trying to find out where he was and when he was expected back."

"Bit unorthodox, if you don't mind me saying so, and now we find ourselves with a second murder on our hands. I use the word murder advisedly as the absence of a weapon from the scene suggests that the death was not suicide."

"I can assure you," said Erwin in his politest voice, "that although the two deaths are undoubtedly connected, we had nothing to do with either of them."

The superintendent shot a quick glance at me. We were all in the library at West Winds and the house was full of police activity. He seemed grudging in his acceptance of the fact that I was probably innocent of Rachel's murder. Erwin had quickly established his bona fide credentials as a journalist without going into the question of why he no longer worked for any of the newspapers, and the superintendent was also quite willing to accept that Belle was his partner in undertaking an attempt to clear me of any suspicion. The policeman had spent his entire career working alongside the press, and none of their activities were capable of surprising him any longer. But the fact remained that two murders had been committed and he had the unenviable task of trying to solve them. He did not relish the thought of some maverick reporter getting in his way.

"I've already spoken to the housekeeper," Haworth went on lugubriously, "and she confirms your story. She says she was with you, Miss Belle, on the stairs when you both heard a sound which she described as a muffled crack and this was followed by an anguished cry and then a loud thud. Upon entering the lounge, the two of you discovered Mr Bland lying on the floor in a deceased state. She also says you both heard the sound of running footsteps which appeared to be coming from outside the house, and that you observed the two French windows were partly open."

Belle nodded her head.

"Turning to you two gentlemen," went on the superintendent, "you claim that you heard footsteps in the road, running up the hill past the spot where you were sitting in your car, and that soon afterwards you believe you heard a vehicle engine starting up."

"It's difficult to be certain," replied Erwin, "because I had pulled the car completely off the road into a small lay-by and we were hidden by trees and hedges. It was also getting quite dark, but I'm sure I heard *somebody* running past on the road although by the time I looked, there was no one to be seen. After all, people do go out running in the evening so it may have been someone local taking a bit of exercise. As for hearing the car starting up, it could have been entirely unconnected. There's a parking place at the bottom of the hill where people occasionally leave their cars to walk along the riverside footpath with their dogs. The tide was out at the time, so it's quite possibly that."

"Bit of a coincidence, nevertheless. Let's move on to my next question. Were any of you acquainted with the deceased?"

"I met him very briefly this morning when I called and spoke to Mrs Seabourne," answered Erwin, "and Godfrey has already told you that he came across him at last weekend's party. Belle, of course, encountered him for a few moments this evening. None of these could be construed as an acquaintance."

"H'm. So on the very evening that the three of you decide to turn up here and conduct your own unofficial inquiry, one of the guests gets himself shot and you expect me to believe that there's no connection?"

"You can believe whatever you like, Superintendent, but that is the truth plain and simple, that's how it is," said Erwin. "Fleet Street may have unorthodox methods, as you like to put it, but journalists do not generally go around arranging for murders to happen. If you ask me my opinion, George Bland was killed because he knew something about Rachel Summers's death and the murderer decided to silence him before he could say anything."

Haworth continued to rub his chin.

"I'll admit it does look a bit that way," he conceded. There was a gentle knock on the library door. "Come in!" he called out.

The door opened and Detective Sergeant Hoskins entered the room.

"Excuse me, sir, but would you mind if I have a word with you?" he said quietly. He took the superintendent to one side and a brief conversation ensued between them in the low well-practised voices of police investigators trying to keep their words confidential. Then Hoskins left the room again and Haworth stood alone for a few moments looking very thoughtful.

"More developments, Superintendent?" said Erwin.

Haworth came slowly back over to us.

"It appears that Charles Seabourne owns a gun," he

said in a measured and contemplative tone, "and it's missing." He looked at us with raised eyebrows. "Do you know anything about this? You seem to know about most things."

Erwin gave a faint smile.

"We *were* aware that he owned a revolver which was apparently handed down to him by his father, and the fact that it's missing does not come as a great surprise. Conclusion – George Bland was shot with Charles Seabourne's gun."

"The press can speculate all it wishes," answered the superintendent in his ponderous way. "The fact that the gun is missing does not necessarily mean that it is the murder weapon. I'm not being drawn on the matter until I've seen the ballistics report."

"Quite so," agreed Erwin, "and I wouldn't expect you to say anything different. All right, let's assume that it was. The only question is – was it kept in a locked or an unlocked drawer? If it was locked, where was the key kept, or was the lock broken? As you can see, superintendent, in the absence of any *official* confirmation, I'm having to make assumptions – I'm assuming that Charles Seabourne's gun was easily available to anyone who knew it was there."

"Dangerous things, assumptions," said Haworth. "I deal only in facts."

Erwin tried a different approach.

"Have you discovered where the gun was fired from? Belle says it sounded muffled so we think the murderer was standing outside the French windows, in which case it was a good shot."

"All in good time. My forensics people are making a thorough search of the grounds and they'll continue to do so tomorrow morning in daylight. In the meantime, there are a number of people I would like to speak to, starting with Mrs Seabourne and her daughter. The doctor's with them at the moment, giving Mrs Seabourne something for shock, but he thinks she'll be all right to answer a few questions. I'll send one of my officers in to take statements off you when he's finished doing Mrs Brown's and then you're free to go."

Superintendent Haworth left the library and we were alone.

"That was a close one," muttered Erwin. "For a minute I didn't think he was going to believe our story."

"It was so far-fetched it couldn't be anything else other than the truth," I replied. "No wonder he's gone, I think you were getting on his nerves, trying to tell him his job."

"That was the idea," he said with a foxy grin. "I've met so many of these senior officers before, and you'll never get anything much out of them, so you've just got to fill in the missing bits and come to your own conclusion. Though fair play to him, I thought he said a lot more to us than he needed to. Anyway," he added, "I think we amateur sleuths are a few moves ahead of him."

"He didn't say anything about letting Godfrey have his car back," said Belle. "I thought that was a cheek."

"He's got more things on his mind than that at the

moment. Besides, he didn't say anything either about charging you with impersonating a gipsy."

"That's because he can't," she answered indignantly. "I am one."

Erwin's face suddenly became serious.

"We can cross George Bland off our list of suspects now," he said. "Poor old George – we never found out much about him, did we? One of the enigmatic types. But his death *must* put him in the position of being one of the key people connected with Rachel's death. If we go back to our original list of those who could have had a motive to murder Rachel, that means that his killer could be Charles or Minkie Seabourne, Jeremy or Catherine, Emma Richmond, Robert Fairweather and last of all James or Julie Carvell. Of those eight, only Minkie and Catherine were here this evening, the rest were all elsewhere."

"When Rosanna and I were going around the house on our search for Charles," said Belle, "there was no sign of Catherine anywhere although her mother told us that she was supposed to be in her room. Rosanna knocked on her bedroom door, but it was empty because we looked in."

Erwin shrugged.

"She might have been in the bathroom, having a shower. She couldn't have been far away because you said she came running quickly enough with all the commotion that occurred after Bland was shot. You said that Minkie rushed into the lounge and became hysterical when she saw him lying dead on the floor."

"Oh, she *did*," said Belle. "She took one look at him and screamed the place down. And then she tried to turn on *me*, as if I'd done it. Said it was all my fault."

"So *why* was George Bland killed?" mused Erwin, smiting his hand against his forehead in concentration. "It *must* have been because he knew something about Rachel's death and had to be silenced. I doubt if you being there at the time had anything to do with it, it would have happened anyway. But wait a minute – let's try and figure this out more carefully. Charles has been gone for a couple of days, supposedly on a business trip, but Rosanna says it's odd because he didn't make his usual arrangements with her about his clean clothes, the sort of things he would pack if he was going to be away from home for a few days. So all right, perhaps he *didn't* go away on a business trip, as we suspected might be the case, because he believed that Rachel's murder had come about as a result of his affair with her. We've already decided that Minkie might have had cause to see this affair as a threat to her position at West Winds, so maybe she decided to murder Rachel..."

"...But got George to carry it out!" I said, finishing off his train of thought. "And in revenge, Charles pretends to go away but stays here all the time in hiding, then at the right time takes his father's old army revolver out of the desk drawer in his study, creeps around the outside of the house and shoots George!"

"And then runs away to the place where he's left his

car," said Belle. "That's what you both hear while you're parked outside waiting for me."

"So that would mean that George Bland followed Rachel back to her home after last Saturday's party and stabbed her to death, leaving her body in the river, and Charles Seabourne, knowing what he had done, shot George dead this evening in the lounge, and now he's in hiding somewhere," concluded Erwin.

"Waiting for his chance to come back and shoot Minkie, too!" I said dramatically. "Because that would be the logical thing to do."

"Yes, it would," agreed Erwin, but then he frowned. "And yet if that was his intention, wouldn't it have been so much easier to kill Minkie at the same time as George? Presumably he knew she was at home, and maybe he was unaware of Belle's visit. If he thinks that Minkie put George up to the job of murdering his beloved Rachel, Minkie is going to be his ultimate target – he's not going to let her get away with it, so by rights she ought to be dead, too. There's something in this that we're missing – I believe we've gone wrong in our reasoning. We're putting the blame on Charles, but why does it *have* to be him? Why not – Jeremy?"

"Or Catherine?" said Belle. "Perhaps we're missing an important detail and Rachel's death has got nothing to do with her affair with Charles, we just *think* it has because it seems the most obvious reason."

"But Catherine was already somewhere in the house so why would she run out afterwards and drive away in a car

210

left some distance up the road? Besides, she couldn't have done that because you said she came quickly into the lounge after the shooting happened."

"All right, let's look at it another way," said Belle, "the running footsteps and the sound of the car starting up were coincidences *not connected* with the shooting of George Bland. Catherine takes the gun from her father's desk drawer, goes around the outside of the house, shoots George and comes straight back into the house, hiding the gun somewhere before pretending to come and see what's happened."

Erwin was not convinced and he shook his head, at the same time drawing a deep breath.

"And yet Catherine must have known that there was a caller – you – so why does she risk carrying out a murder when there's a visitor on the premises? No, that won't do. You might as well suggest that Minkie shot George Bland. If mother or daughter were thinking of killing him, they'd do it when the house was empty. Surely, at a time when Rosanna wasn't around either. Let's go back to our original list of suspects, because we also need to consider Emma Richmond – who admittedly seems a very unlikely culprit – James and Julie Carvell – James by his own admission had a brief affair with Rachel – and Robert Fairweather. Just suppose that George Bland *didn't* have anything to do with Rachel's murder but knew who *had* done it and was *blackmailing* them."

"In other words," I said, "we're no nearer to knowing the truth than we were before. George Bland's death tells us precisely *nothing*."

"No, no, it tells us *everything*, but with a vital detail still missing, we're failing to understand the real significance of it. I'm sure something has already been said that gives us that important missing clue."

The door of the library opened and Detective Sergeant Hoskins looked in momentarily. He was holding some papers in his hand.

"The superintendent has asked me to take your statements," he said soberly. "I'll be with you in five minutes and when that's done, he says you're free to go."

Erwin began prowling restlessly around the room, talking to himself. The few words I could hear him muttering were: "There *must* be a common denominator that provides the missing clue – and it's probably something we already know about."

Belle had decided to give the matter a rest and started to browse through the bookshelves to see if she could find anything to her taste. She had a liking for romantic fiction – prince elopes with peasant girl, that kind of thing – but doubted if she would come across any books of that sort. There was a large collection of financial publications, which she found rather boring, and big heavy volumes on history, geography and philosophy. She also discovered a row of books on sailing, and picked one out to have a look at it.

After reading through it for a while and admiring the pictures of old-fashioned yachts and pleasure boats from years ago, she said out loud to us: "There's a very interesting book here about coastal waterways. It's got a lot of old photographs in it from around here. You'd hardly recognise what Saltcombe was like a hundred years ago."

I noticed that Erwin was staring at her with a strange expression on his face, as if something that had been puzzling him was now revealed in all its clarity.

"Of course!" he said at last. "I can see now what should have been obvious! There *is* a common denominator which may provide us with the missing clue – the *Sarah Jane!*"

19

I Go Aboard The *Sarah Jane* Again

Half an hour later, our statements to the police having been taken by the redoubtable Detective Sergeant Hoskins, Erwin, Belle and I were allowed to leave West Winds. The place was still teeming with police activity and probably would be for some time to come. Outside on the driveway stood a dark van marked with the words "Private Ambulance" waiting to remove George Bland's body to the mortuary. Instead of returning to Erwin's car, we left it parked where it was and walked down the road to the bottom of the hill where, in the darkness, we found the footpath that led to the riverbank and stumbled our way along it until we reached the small wooden jetty used by the Seabournes to get out to the *Sarah Jane*. The cabin cruiser was moored in its usual place in the middle of the river but low water was approaching so the boat was settled on the sandbank, barely afloat. It was clearly visible in the moonlight. Erwin had earlier brought a small torch from the car and put it in his pocket, and now he shone it around the jetty. I had already told him about the small inflatable dinghy that Jeremy had used to get on board, but on that occasion the *Sarah Jane* had been fully afloat and in a manoeuvrable state. Erwin dismissed the idea of using the dinghy and was now sizing up the depth of the river in consideration of wading across.

"Should be safe enough," was his opinion, "if neither of you minds getting your feet wet."

We took off our boots and shoes and Belle gathered up her long skirt while Erwin and I both rolled up our trousers, and we carefully lowered ourselves down from the jetty into the cold water, treading on mud one minute and pebbles the next. It went from being very squelchy to extremely uncomfortable. Erwin led the way, as this expedition was all his doing, with Belle in the middle and myself bringing up the rear, all of us holding hands for safety. We splashed our way across the rippling water of the outgoing tide and scrambled on board. The boat was slightly tilted to one side and the list would become more pronounced as the river became increasingly shallow.

"Let's go below," said Erwin quietly, and went down half a dozen steps into the tiny cabin. Only then did he switch on his torch again and shone it around, taking care to avoid the light showing through the portholes and being noticed on land. It was rather eerie, exploring the interior of the boat by torchlight, for it cast long dark moving shadows, and we heard the continuous hollow sound of water lapping against the bottom of the hull. Two empty bottles of champagne were still lying on one of the berths, where they had been carelessly thrown last

Saturday night, together with the glasses, and on the floor of the cabin was a box containing more unopened bottles, together with coiled up lengths of rope and a marlinspike that glinted in the light. Erwin bent down with his back to Belle and myself to rummage among the items, and then he turned around and glanced at me.

"Brings back memories?" he said in a low voice.

I nodded, thinking of the last time I had been on board, standing out on deck with Rachel by my side, and the happy carefree atmosphere of the evening. I could almost hear the ghostly echo of our voices.

"Tell me again," said Erwin. "I think it could be very important."

I drew a deep breath and thought back to the evening that now seemed caught up in some kind of unreal limbo, almost as if it had never happened but might instead have been nothing more than a dream. Where should I begin? At last I gathered my recollections into the order in which they occurred. I needed to do it for Rachel's sake, and to do it properly.

"It must have been halfway through the evening," I began slowly, "and I remember that Rachel and I had gone out into the front garden of West Winds, where lots of the other guests were standing around with their drinks, talking. We were on our own, separate from everyone else to begin with, until Catherine took Rachel over to where Jeremy and Emma were standing. I seem to recall that George Bland was not far away, looking at the view towards the river. Rachel came back soon afterwards, full of excitement, saying that somebody had suggested going out in the *Sarah Jane* before it got dark for a bit of fun."

"Can you remember whose idea it was?" asked Erwin, looking at me keenly in the torchlight.

"No, she didn't say, but for some reason I assumed it was Jeremy. Well, it *would* be, wouldn't it, surely? I remember asking Rachel if she thought it would be safe to go, because Emma had raised some concerns about it in the pub two nights earlier. She'd said that it was supposed to be leaking, and the engine didn't work properly. But Rachel didn't seem bothered about it, saying that the idea wouldn't have been suggested if the boat were unsafe and likely to sink or break down. So we went. It was rather strange, actually, because I had this thought in my mind of it being like a scene from the past, in the days when boating was all the rage for rich young people, and it was as if what we were planning to do was a throwback to the past. So to begin with we had Jeremy and Emma, Catherine, Rachel and myself, and we were joined by Robert Fairweather and James and Julie Carvell. As we got ready to go, George Bland seemed to be watching us with a slightly envious, almost anxious, look on his face as though he wanted to come along as well, but he stayed up at the house. We set off down the path from the garden to the road lower down the hill, crossed it and then followed the towpath to the jetty, like we did just now. Jeremy took the dinghy over to the *Sarah Jane* and brought her across to the jetty, where we all got on board. Robert jumped on last of all because he was holding the mooring line, and then we cast off and set course for Saltcombe."

"Whose idea was that?" asked Erwin.

"What?"

"To go to Saltcombe?"

I had to think for a minute.

"It was James," I said at last. "He mentioned it. But where else would we have gone?"

Erwin shrugged.

"I suppose you could have headed up the river instead of down it."

"Possibly, but how far up does the river reach?"

"Quite a long way – it twists and turns, but it's navigable when there's a high tide."

"Well anyway, I remember Jeremy saying that we had plenty of time because high water wasn't until quarter-past one, or something like that. We all settled back to enjoy the trip, with Jeremy at the helm."

"Downstream would certainly give him more scope to show off," conceded Erwin. "You mentioned champagne," he reminded me, pointing to the empty bottles on the bunk.

"Yes, Robert came below and suddenly reappeared on deck holding two bottles, and everyone got very excited because it wasn't expected."

"And yet," said Erwin thoughtfully, "the bottles were already on board – look in that box, there's another six of them – even though you're saying that the trip was spontaneously decided upon only a few minutes earlier up at the house. That seems a bit odd, doesn't it?"

"Perhaps they always keep a supply of champagne on the boat," suggested Belle brightly, "for just such an eventuality."

"Possibly," agreed Erwin slowly. "Possibly. Go on with the story."

"There was a lot of drinking good health to everyone, and that was when Jeremy must have lost concentration for a few seconds because the boat gave a sudden lurch, as if it had either hit something or got caught in some rough water. Robert almost fell back into the cabin, and you should have seen the look on his face – he wasn't in the least bit amused! All the jollity stopped at that point and Jeremy became more serious. We sailed down as far as Saltcombe, by which time it was beginning to get quite dark, so we turned around and came back."

"And after that? Once you got ashore?"

"We waited on the jetty for Jeremy to put the boat back on its mooring – I remember being very impressed at the way he handled the boathook and the mooring line in the dark – and then once he came back on dry land, he and Catherine started telling us the tale of how their father had bought the *Sarah Jane* many years earlier from someone in Henley-on-Thames and sailed it all the way back to Watersford single-handed. It seems that it was a very rough passage in the English Channel and they said he was lucky to make it. That gave Robert the excuse to start going on about wooden boats again, which is his pet subject – and then Rachel said a curious thing. She described it as being very odd. She said she noticed something earlier, but it was probably her imagination. When the boat lurched in the water and nearly caused Robert to lose his balance, he grabbed hold of a handrail, but she said that when she used to go out on the *Sarah Jane* with Jeremy, she couldn't remember the rail being there, she thought it was in a different position. Let me show you – it's this one here."

I pointed to the handrail on the deck outside the cabin, and Erwin tentatively shone the torch on it, cupping his one hand over the beam to prevent it from being seen on land. He examined the mounting brackets and studied the bulkhead to which it was attached.

"It doesn't look to me as though it's been moved at all," he said. "In any case, why would it be?"

"Rachel dismissed it as if it weren't of any importance," I replied. "Anyway, those are the main points I remember of the evening." I omitted to mention our passionate few moments beside the footpath on the way back up to the house.

"H'm," said Erwin pensively. "If I'm right about the *Sarah Jane* being the common denominator, is there anything in your account that points to something of particular interest, I wonder?"

The three of us were standing out on the sloping deck again, feeling the fresh cool evening breeze blowing against our faces. Clouds were passing fitfully over the moon, making for short periods of complete darkness, and longer periods when the surrounding countryside was bathed in its pale illumination. We already knew that the *Sarah Jane's* mooring could not be seen from West Winds, and it was equally apparent that there were few places on the Watersford side of the river from where it would be visible. It was possible to see it from part of the tidal road, and Erwin's eyes scanned the dark mass of land keenly to determine if there was anywhere else from where it could be seen. And then he tensed suddenly, as though he had found what he was searching for.

"Look!" he said, pointing into the darkness. "Over there in the distance. Can you see what I mean? Above those trees."

Belle and I followed the direction of his outstretched arm, trying to discover what he was pointing at.

"I can't see anything," protested Belle, peering hard.

"Nor can I," I said in agreement with her, until some small detail caught my attention. "No, wait – there *is* a light over there, above the trees. It's a building, and there are more dark shapes to the side of it."

"Exactly," said Erwin softly. "And do you know where it is? It's Skylark Farm. That faint bit of brightness you can see is a light coming from the farmhouse, and one of those buildings to the side of it is, I imagine, the stable."

"You mean—"

"I mean Rachel could see the *Sarah Jane* from up there at her farm."

"But it was dark!"

"Yes, but she would be familiar enough with the

position of the boat in daylight, knowing that it was always tied up in the same place on the river, so what if she had her attention drawn to it in the dark *by someone on board shining a light*. That's the only explanation – she couldn't make it out any other way, even in moonlight. She sees something that makes her suspicious and comes down to investigate. We know there's a track that leads straight down from the farm to the tidal road, because that's the way she used to ride her horse – you told me about it yourself."

"But the tide would have been almost fully in at that time," said Belle.

"And she was discovered without any shoes on," Erwin reminded us. "Perhaps she came down the track and took off her shoes when she reached the water. Last Saturday it would be almost a neap tide – in other words, the lowest of the high tides – so the water may never have been any higher than her knees, and probably quite a bit less than that. From there, carrying her shoes in one hand, she might have followed the tidal road, knowing it perfectly well even in the dark when it was flooded by the river, and if she was determined to do so, she could have walked all the way along it, keeping between the wooden marker posts, until she reached the towpath. That would then have brought her to the jetty, at which point she would be able to see the *Sarah Jane* very clearly – even in the darkness."

Erwin paused to allow us to consider the implications of what he had said. The silence was only broken by the sound of the outgoing tide, splashing quietly against the bottom of the boat.

"It all fits in with what we already know," I said at length.

"But it still leaves one very important question unanswered," went on Erwin. "If Rachel's attention was initially drawn by a light shining on board the boat, which she saw from the stable whilst she was checking her horse before going to bed, who *was* it on the *Sarah Jane* – and what were they doing?"

With that intriguing question in mind, we decided there was nothing more we could achieve by staying on board, so we prepared to make our way back to the riverbank.

Erwin told Belle and myself to go on ahead.

"I just want to look in the cabin one last time," he added. "I'll catch up with you."

I helped Belle to clamber over the side and we dropped silently into the flowing river, feeling the cold water against our bare legs. We both gave an involuntary gasp with the sudden shock of it touching our skin. The water level had fallen to its lowest point in the time we had been on the boat, and the *Sarah Jane* was now fully grounded. We steadied each other by holding hands and waded slowly towards the jetty. Glancing back over my shoulder, I saw Erwin's shadowy figure come back up on deck and drop quietly into the river. He had almost caught up with us by the time we reached dry land, and we stood on the jetty, shivering in the chilly night air but with a feeling of satisfaction that we had accomplished something worthwhile. Erwin was in a particularly cheerful mood.

"Let's get back to the car," he said. "This little excursion has made several things a lot clearer to me. I intend to return at dawn, when it will be light enough to see the *Sarah Jane* better."

Belle's skirt was quite wet, and so were our trousers, despite having kept them rolled up for the crossing of the river, but we managed to put our damp feet into our boots and shoes and made our way back to where the car was parked in its small lay-by up the hill. The water had cleared completely from the tidal road but Erwin still drove the car slowly and carefully through the damp weed-strewn surface and we got back to Watersford without incident. He turned up the lane and stopped outside Hill Cottage for me to get out and we agreed to meet again at eight o'clock the following morning.

"I'll call for you and we'll take a walk down there, as if we were just out for an early morning stroll," he said. "The tide will be going out again by then, so the boat will be barely afloat. After we've had a look at it, we need to go up to the farm in order to confirm my suspicion that the *Sarah Jane* is visible from there."

I gave my assent to the plan and got out of the car. Erwin and Belle drove off back to their place and I went indoors to spend a restless night, wondering what the next day would bring in the way of new developments.

20

I Witness A Disappearance

The following morning dawned bright and clear, and I rose early enough to make breakfast and still have time to tidy everything away afterwards before there was a knock on the front door to announce Erwin's arrival.

"Belle's fast asleep," he said. "She was very tired after the excitement of yesterday evening."

"I didn't have a particularly good night's rest," I replied. "My mind was too busy trying to figure everything out."

"Same here. I paced up and down for most of the night, but it was time well spent. I think I have an idea what happened."

"Erwin! Do you mean you've solved it?"

"Not exactly – there are still a few details I'm not very clear about, but I'm almost there."

"That's wonderful news! Can you tell me who you think did it?"

He hesitated.

"I'd rather not at the moment. As in all good detective stories, I'd prefer to keep it to myself because I don't want to say anything yet in case I'm wrong. Remember that there are still two people we haven't spoken to."

"Charles and Jeremy?"

"Yes, and they are two of the most important witnesses. If Superintendent Haworth is thinking along the same lines as me, he'll be moving heaven and earth to try and find them – Charles especially – so perhaps we ought to let him do our job for us in that respect."

"If he finds Charles, I imagine the first thing he'll be doing is arresting him on suspicion of shooting George Bland, so that won't give you much chance to talk to him. *You'd* have to find him first, and risk getting yourself shot."

"That is possible, although somehow I don't think he'll be shooting me," said Erwin slowly and cryptically. "Anyway, let's get started. A good brisk early morning walk won't do us any harm but I recommend a good pair of wellingtons, like these."

He had come suitably dressed for walking in the river and I took his advice and went into the small storage room behind the kitchen where the absentee owners of the cottage, assuming that they were going to rent it out as holiday accommodation and were planning to stay there themselves from time to time, had left a lot of angling equipment and plenty of wet weather clothes in anticipation of doing some river fishing. The outdoor clothing included waterproofs, waders and two pairs of wellington boots. One pair fitted me, more or less, so I put them on and joined Erwin in the living room.

"Good," he said, satisfied, "let's go."

We stepped out of Hill Cottage and set off along the narrow lane that led eventually to the tidal road, which, for the last hundred yards, was approached down a steep wooded hillside. At the bottom, we emerged onto the road, still well covered in places by the outgoing tide, with the usual deposits of green slimy waterweed which it was best to avoid stepping on. All was quiet at eight o'clock in the morning, with no other walkers about and traffic barely able to make its way along the road, and we headed in the direction of Saltcombe, its ultimate destination. It was a beautiful sunny morning with a clear blue sky overhead and a fringe of fine weather cumulus clouds on the horizon. We would only have to walk a distance of less than a mile along the partly-flooded road before we reached the bend that led uphill past West Winds, at which point we could gain access to the riverside towpath.

We knew, however, that the *Sarah Jane* should become visible to us well before we got that far along the road, for it could always be seen fleetingly in its position along the river's meandering course through a gap in the trees, and when it failed to appear in view, as expected, a look of grave concern crossed Erwin's face.

"That's odd," he said. "We should be able to see it from here." He pointed ahead. "See? Through there."

We stopped at the side of the road. Other small boats were in their usual positions, moored in the middle of the river. They were mostly small motor boats but there were one or two yachts amongst them, their tall masts pointing skywards. They were a familiar sight, moored in the same place each day but invariably turned in slightly different directions from one day to the next according to the movement of the receding water. There was no sign of the *Sarah Jane*, which we should have been able to see by now, even though we were still some distance from its mooring.

"Perhaps I'm mistaken," muttered Erwin. "Maybe it's further down where you can see it."

We set off again at a quickened pace, but the river was conspicuously empty at the spot where the cabin cruiser should have been. We kept going, splashing through shallow water, passing the wooden marker posts at the edge of the road where the river was joined by one of its small tributaries, and soon we had reached the bend where the road began to run inland and turned off along the riverbank footpath. By now it was plainly evident that the *Sarah Jane* was no longer at her mooring – the big round red float lay alone on the water.

"I should have thought of that!" exclaimed Erwin, and cursed himself in frustration and annoyance. "Why *didn't* I think of it?"

I stared at him, feeling confused.

"Why didn't you think of what? And who do you think has taken it? The police?"

"No! If the police were interested in it, they'd examine it where it was, at least to begin with, and there would be a big cordon around it. No, indeed, it's not the police who've taken it but someone else with a much more sinister reason, unless I'm very much mistaken."

"You believe that Charles has come back for it?"

"Well, after all, it *is* his boat." He lapsed into deep thought and began muttering to himself. "So it was taken in the early hours of the morning, but where did it go? Was it moved upstream or downstream? It would surely need to be hidden away somewhere, and there wouldn't be many places to do that upstream, except for one or two tiny narrow creeks. No, it must have gone down the river towards Saltcombe. Maybe even out to sea. Oh, what a fool I was last night not to foresee this happening!" He gave an explosive sigh of despair and turned to me. "I've *got* to find it, if there's to be any hope of solving Rachel's murder, and that of George Bland."

"But you already said you have an idea what happened."

"Godfrey, let me explain – this is a puzzle with a lot of different pieces, or clues, and from the way those pieces – the clues – are fitting together, I'm beginning to see the overall picture, but the biggest clue of all is the *Sarah Jane*, and now it's missing. Well, *I've got to find it!*"

I stared long and hard into Erwin's eyes.

"Is there something you haven't told me?"

He merely gave a crooked smile.

"There might be one or two details I've kept back from you," he admitted, "because I don't want to influence your mind with an incorrect theory if I happen to be wrong. In the event that I *am* mistaken, your own thoughts will remain unaffected – provided they haven't been led in the wrong direction by my telling you what those details are. Do you understand?"

"Yes, but when, in that case, *will* you be able to tell me?" I asked plaintively.

"Once I have obtained that final incontrovertible piece of evidence. There's nothing to be gained by staying here any longer, let's walk back to your place."

"Come and have a cup of tea or coffee," I invited.

"Good idea. Let's go."

He threw a final glance at the empty stretch of river, now approaching low water, and it was obvious that he had hoped to wade across and carry out a further examination of the Seabournes' boat, only to be thwarted by an unexpected turn of events. And yet by his own admission, Erwin said that he should have foreseen the possibility, so what did he mean by that? We walked back in silence, and my mind tried to work it out for myself. If it were Charles Seabourne who had shot George Bland – as seemed most likely – perhaps he decided that the best way of evading the law was to flee in his own boat. He was, after all, a highly competent sailor by all accounts and could probably take it anywhere he wanted – the weather was fine so it would be easy enough to sail across the English Channel to the continent.

We were assuming, of course, that it *was* Charles who had killed Bland. What if we were wrong? It was equally possible that Jeremy had taken the *Sarah Jane* and not his father. Did that point to Jeremy being the murderer? It was perfectly feasible that he had taken his father's gun from the desk in the study. Neither Charles nor Jeremy was presently at home, making it impossible to verify either man's movements. But why would Jeremy want to kill George Bland? Perhaps in his case there was a less obvious motive.

My mind tried to grapple with the problem on our return walk along the tidal road, and Erwin was equally deep in thought. Nearing Watersford, I noticed another early riser, a local man paddling across the river in a tiny rubber dinghy to get to his small boat which was lying in deeper water near the road bridge. It was called *Poppy*. There was another similar boat close by, bearing the name *Skipper*. They were used for fishing, and had outboard motors. The man I was idly watching probably intended going out before low water but he was carrying a toolbox in his dinghy so I guessed that he had some work to do. Perhaps the motor needed fixing.

"That's the sort of little boat I wouldn't mind having," I said, breaking the long silence. "Over there."

Erwin looked up.

"What's that?" he replied.

"I've always wanted my own little boat. See those two over there? That fellow in the dinghy must be going out to one of them. I assume he knows which is his – they both look the same to me!"

Erwin turned his gaze to look where I was pointing. The man had reached one of the boats and was struggling to lift his toolbox over the side.

"Oh yes," he said distractedly, "I see what you mean. He obviously knows his own boat."

We carried on walking for a few more moments and then suddenly Erwin broke his stride and paused to glance back at the man who, with the effort of what he was doing, almost toppled headlong into *Poppy* and had to turn quickly to grab hold of the dinghy before it floated away. Erwin's face broke into an ironic smile at the sight of it.

"Can't see for the life of me how you'd get any enjoyment out of doing that," he said laconically.

"It's the idea of being free to go wherever you want," I explained, "and the sense of adventure that goes with it."

"Well, it looks like a lot of hard work to me. I mean, what's the man doing now?"

I peered across the stretch of water.

"He seems to be taking the cover off the outboard motor," I said. "Perhaps it's not working properly."

"So what happens if it breaks down when you're out at sea?"

"Then you radio for help."

"And if the radio isn't working?"

"That's why you're meant to carry distress flares."

"Which might be out of date."

I shrugged. There was clearly no satisfying Erwin.

"Well, of course there's always a chance of a mishap," I conceded, "and I imagine most boat owners accept that. Yes, all right, people *are* lost at sea – it can easily happen to the most experienced sailor, but you don't let that small chance stop you from doing what you really want to do."

Erwin shook his head sadly, as if he completely failed to comprehend how anyone could want to mess about on the water, and then his expression quickly changed to one of surprise and then contemplation – a thought had occurred to him, a vague idea that seemed, at first, nonsensical and bizarre until he turned it over again in his mind and everything became clear.

21

I Learn Of Jeremy's Return

A handwritten note was waiting for us when we got back to Hill Cottage. It was scribbled on a small scrap of paper and placed in the letterbox on the front door. I pulled it out and read the message. It said simply: Jeremy's back – Belle.

I showed it to Erwin.

"Belle must have heard from Rosanna," he said in a tone of satisfaction, pleased that the Seabournes' housekeeper had kept her promise to let him know of any important developments. "That's good. Let's forget about the cup of tea or coffee and go straight back to my place."

We continued walking, this time at a faster pace, along the lane in the direction of Watersford village and soon came to Erwin's little tin bungalow. Belle must have been watching out for us because she opened the front door immediately.

"I've had a phone call from Rosanna," she said breathlessly. "Jeremy arrived back at West Winds during the night and the police have been speaking to him ever since!"

Erwin gave Belle an appreciative kiss and we all went inside and made our way to the living room. Erwin was evidently preoccupied with deciding what to do. He waved a hand for me to sit down in an armchair and carried on pacing up and down the room restlessly.

"I've *got* to speak to him – but how?" he was saying, and then he turned to Belle. "No news of Charles?"

She shook her head.

"Did Rosanna say where Jeremy's been?"

"No, but apparently he arrived in a car she hasn't seen before so she *thinks* he's been up in London – it's not unusual for him to bring different cars back from the showroom. And she said the police have been puzzled by the fact that George Bland's car is not at the house, although it is quite possible that Jeremy drove it back to London."

"What *is* going on?" muttered Erwin, and I could see a puzzled look returning to his face, as if some of his previously held assumptions were being challenged.

"Let me get you a cup of tea," said Belle helpfully, and disappeared into the kitchen for a few minutes whilst I sat quietly in the corner, not daring to say a word in case it interrupted his thoughts. Belle carried two cups of steaming hot tea into the room and handed one of them to me, putting the other down on the table.

Erwin came to a decision.

"Be a love and ring Rosanna back," he said to Belle,

"and tell her that I *must* speak to Jeremy – it's imperative. There has to be a way of doing so, even if the place is crawling with police. He won't know me, of course, but he *has* met Godfrey. Explain the position to her and say that I don't want Superintendent Haworth to know I'm there – can she suggest anything? She's a resourceful woman and it's a very large house."

Belle nodded and went into the hallway, where an ancient telephone was standing on a shelf and looked as if it had been there from the earliest days of dialling, although it was in pristine condition on account of Belle being a particularly house-proud woman: she must have spent ages at some time or other cleaning and polishing the black Bakelite. Soon we heard her voice talking to someone, interspersed by a few pauses. The conversation seemed to go on for a long time but eventually we heard her replace the receiver and she came back into the room.

"I hate speaking to policemen," she said, pulling a face. "They make me feel guilty before I've even said anything. One of the superintendent's men answered the telephone so I said I wanted to speak to Mrs Brown the housekeeper – I pretended to be a friend of hers with an urgent message – and he went to get her. Anyway, when she came on the line I told her exactly what you had said about needing to see Jeremy alone without the superintendent knowing. She said it might be a bit difficult because he's been with the police most of the time since he's been back, although in the last few minutes she's seen him on his own and it seems he's been told not to leave the house. She said that as he already knows Godfrey, she will tell him that you, Godfrey, have something very important to see him about, and that you're bringing a friend along with you. Go to the summerhouse in the garden and she'll tell him to meet you there in fifteen minutes. You can get to the summerhouse without having to go anywhere near the main drive – there's a path that leads from the front garden down to the river – and that means you won't be seen from the house."

"I know it," I said immediately. "That's the same path that we used last night to go down to the boat."

"Which," said Erwin, looking meaningfully at Belle, "has disappeared."

"What's disappeared?" she replied blankly.

"The *Sarah Jane*. Since last night, it's gone. Vanished. Been taken from its mooring. Things are beginning to happen very quickly, and rather too unexpectedly for my liking."

"So you didn't get to see it again this morning?"

"No, but I saw something else instead, and I think that was just as significant." Erwin clapped his hands together in anticipation. "Right, let's go! We've got quarter of an hour to get over to West Winds. Come on, Godfrey, I need you to show me where this summerhouse is. Let's find out what Jeremy has to say for himself!"

Fifteen minutes barely gave us enough time to walk back down the tidal road so Erwin got the car out into the lane and we set off in that, stopping briefly at Hill

Cottage for me to change back from wellington boots into shoes. As Erwin wanted to avoid the possibility of the car being seen from West Winds, he pulled it off the road onto the grass verge just before we reached the now drying-out stretch of road that had the wooden marker posts. We covered the last few hundred yards on foot and I directed him to the small wooden gate set in the lower garden wall which gave access to the path that led up to the front garden. Without saying a word, in case the sound of our voices was heard by anyone in the grounds, meaning police officers, we ascended the steep path that came out on the front lawn and hid behind some large bushes which kept us safely hidden from view.

I tapped Erwin on the shoulder and pointed.

"The summerhouse is over there on the far side of the house," I whispered in his ear. "And on this side," I pointed to our left, "the driveway comes up and finishes in a big parking area, but the garage is around the back, out of sight. Let's see if we can make our way over in that direction behind these trees." I indicated to the right, where a line of tall sycamores provided an effective natural screen. The lawn was also bordered by lots of small ornamental bushes and these likewise provided a generous amount of cover as we edged our way around the front of the house without revealing ourselves. There was no sign of anyone in the garden so I guessed that all of the police activity was concentrated inside the main building, but this was not the time to put any assumptions to the test. I did not fancy coming face to face with Superintendent Haworth or Sergeant Hoskins, or indeed any of the forensics people who were still undoubtedly carrying out a minute examination of the premises.

The summerhouse came into view on the far side of the house, situated in a small secluded garden of its own, with stone statues and a low wall decorated with classical pillars. The doors of the summerhouse were open, revealing an interior furnished with comfortable cushioned loungers and a table. Erwin and I cautiously approached it across the lawn, but the house was well hidden from view so there was little chance of our being seen, and we walked across a raised verandah and entered; as we did so, a tall figure stepped unexpectedly out of the shadows in the far corner and made us both jump with surprise.

"What exactly is the meaning of all this?" demanded Jeremy Seabourne in a sharp, angry voice. "I've spent all morning being questioned by the police, and now Rosanna comes and tells me that *you* want to see me about something very important. You of all people! And who's *this*?" He shifted his gaze away from me and inclined his head towards Erwin.

"I'm sorry this has had to be done in a somewhat dramatic fashion," I said apologetically, feeling rather clumsy, "but I'd like to introduce you to Erwin Graham who wants to have a word with you."

"Who the hell's Erwin Graham? I don't know you, do I?" he said aggressively, turning his attention fully to

Erwin, who responded with a thin smile. "I mean to say, what *is* going on around here? I arrive home early this morning to be met at the door by a policeman who tells me that George has been shot in our lounge and is dead. And as for you," his eyes came back to rest on me again, "I thought it was *you* the police wanted to question about Rachel's murder!"

"I think we need to straighten a few things out," said Erwin quietly and soothingly. "I'm a journalist covering the murder of Rachel Summers so my investigation is not of an official nature, I'm doing it for a newspaper. The police are fully aware of who I am and I've been working on the story from the moment Rachel's body was found." I had to admire his ability to lie with such plausible conviction, and I'm quite certain I would have believed every word of it myself if I had been in Jeremy Seabourne's position. "Since last Monday I have spoken to all of the key witnesses who knew Rachel and were at your parents' house party on the weekend. All, that is, except you and your father."

Jeremy stared at us sullenly.

"Dad's been away on business since Sunday evening and my mother doesn't know when he's due back. There's no mystery about where *I've* been. George asked me to take the Porsche that he had come down in last Friday back up to London, then I did a couple of days' work while I was there and brought another car back late last night. By the time the police say they were starting to look for me, I was already on my way down here."

"Is there any way you can prove your whereabouts yesterday evening at around half-past eight?" asked Erwin.

Jeremy began spluttering.

"Are you trying to accuse *me* of shooting George?" he retorted incredulously.

"It's hardly an unreasonable question. I'm merely asking you if you can."

"Well as a matter of fact, yes, I have a petrol receipt from a filling station on the journey out of London," said Jeremy with a look of triumph on his face. "And the police seem quite satisfied." He finished with a nod of the head, which was his unspoken way of saying "So there!"

"And does there happen to be an equally verifiable way you can prove your whereabouts on the night Rachel was murdered?"

This time, Jeremy's expression faltered and the bold thrust of his chin diminished.

"I – I was with Emma," he replied.

"Your fiancée?"

"Yes, we're due to get married next spring."

"And she will no doubt be able to back you up on that?"

"Of course she will!"

Erwin seemed less than satisfied.

"When I spoke to her and asked her what she did on Saturday night after the party she seemed a bit hesitant."

"What do you mean, hesitant?"

"As if she couldn't remember what she did, or whether

she was with you. And if you'll forgive me for saying so, you even seemed a bit uncertain yourself a few moments ago."

"Damn it all, we were together the whole evening!"

"And at the end? Did she go home to Kingsbridge or did she stay at West Winds?" Erwin looked keenly at Jeremy for any further sign of hesitancy.

Jeremy must have sensed that his evasiveness was casting a less than convincing light over his explanation. "She stayed," he said at last, and let out a long sigh. "We spent the night together at West Winds. But, as it happens, she *did* want to go home. We'd had a slight difference of opinion, nothing very much, and she said she wanted to go back to her place in Kingsbridge. In the end I managed to persuade her to stay. The tide was in so the road was flooded and that would have meant a long detour, and we'd both had a few to drink so that would have meant calling for a taxi. So she stayed."

"Reluctantly?"

"We *are* entitled to have occasional arguments, you know!"

"Was it about Rachel?"

Jeremy became silent and a strange look flickered across his face. He glanced quickly at me.

"Well, yes, actually it was," he murmured in a low voice.

"Because she was your ex-fiancée and Emma didn't like having her around?"

Jeremy stared at Erwin, clearly taken aback by the

directness of the question.

"I don't know," he said, shaking his head slowly. "I thought they got on all right with each other, there didn't seem to be any animosity between them."

"Mr Seabourne," said Erwin sternly, as if he were addressing a young child, "you don't seriously expect me to believe that you thought you could put Emma Richmond, the young woman to whom you are presently engaged to be married, in the same room as Rachel Summers, the young woman to whom you *used* to be engaged, and there not to be serious discord! But let us not argue about that point, because I have a far more important question to ask you. Have you any idea who might have wanted to kill Rachel?"

"Of course not!" retorted Jeremy. "If I knew, I'd say!"

Erwin held his gaze steadily.

"There have been two murders in the space of four days," he said in a voice that was icy cold, "and they both involve people who were known to your family. Rachel Summers, your ex-fiancée, was also – to put it bluntly – your father's mistress, and George Bland was his business associate. Mr Bland was shot and your father's revolver is missing."

"W-what are you trying to suggest?"

"Where is your father at this moment?"

"I've already told you, he's away on business! Look, I don't know what you're trying to achieve with these questions, but not even the superintendent spoke to me in the way you are."

"Then perhaps he should have done," said Erwin evenly. "Two murders, Mr Seabourne, and you're trying to make out that they've got nothing to do with you or your family. Frankly, I find that hard to believe. Now, may I continue?"

Jeremy passed his tongue nervously over his lips.

"If you must."

"Were you aware of the relationship between Rachel and your father?"

Jeremy took a deep breath and let out a despairing sigh.

"Yes! Yes, of course I was aware of it! Everyone in the family knew about it – even Catherine, who tried to pretend otherwise. She and Rachel had been friends since they were very young, so Rachel started coming back and fore to this house years ago. We more or less grew up together, although I was several years older than her. She was twenty when we started going out, the two of us, and we soon fell in love. It seemed strange at first, having a deep emotional feeling for each other, given that we'd grown up together as children, but there you are – it happened. We got engaged, and she often came up to London to stay in my little flat in Kensington. You'd have thought we were the perfect young couple, and of course Rachel was absolutely stunning to look at, especially when she took the trouble to get dressed up." He smiled at the recollection and then shrugged his shoulders. "But it didn't last. I was very keen on the social life of the big city with its pubs and night clubs and Rachel, in spite of all her outward show of sophistication, preferred the quiet life here in Devon. It also seems that she had a liking for other men, and I was shocked to discover that my father was one of them."

"Was that before or after you broke off the engagement?"

"I found out before, and we had a big row about it. She denied it, and so did my father, but we all knew."

"She was, I understand, expecting a baby, but lost it?" said Erwin gently.

"You know about that, too?"

Erwin nodded.

"Dear God, what an unholy mess it had become," went on Jeremy. "There was my father, having an affair with my fiancée who happened also to be my sister's best friend and there was she, expecting his child! Well, it certainly wasn't mine, anyway. He was very excited at the prospect of having a second family, until the miscarriage."

"How did he take it?"

"Oh, terribly. The family thought it would bring him to his senses, but if anything, it made him worse."

"If Rachel hadn't died, do you think your parents would have divorced?"

"I don't know. Probably not. I think my father wanted a mistress as well as a wife and saw the two as being mutually compatible, like they do in France. I don't think he had any moral qualms about it. He and my mother are no longer very close emotionally, and haven't been for some time, despite appearances, but a divorce would prove much too costly for him. This wasn't his first affair, and I doubt if it will be his last."

"Do you think he had anything to do with Rachel's death?"

"Why? What reason would he have to want to harm her?"

"Perhaps he was jealous. After all, he saw her arrive at his house-party with Godfrey on her arm."

Jeremy had a defiant gleam in his eye.

"Well, you'll have to ask him when you see him!"

"I would very much like to, Mr Seabourne," said Erwin. "Believe me, I would very much like to. Changing the subject, tell me about George Bland – how long have you known him?"

"All my life. I still can't believe he's dead as well. George has been – was – a very close friend of my father's for many years. They met a long time ago through business – George and his wife began coming down to stay at least once a year, usually in the summer. He's a property developer – he owns properties all over the country – and he was interested in buying a hotel in Saltcombe. For the last three or four years he's been down here quite regularly, staying over the weekend, usually when my parents have organised a do, mostly on his own, and apparently he's been trying to persuade James and Julie to sell him their guest house. They were going through a difficult period financially not long ago, but they stuck it out and kept it running. Every time he was down, he'd get into a huddle with James, and although it was James's parents who originally owned it, Julie was the one who told him they wouldn't sell it at any price. It became a bit of a joke actually – if George is coming down, expect a higher offer!"

Erwin smiled.

"He obviously wanted to be a seaside landlord," he said politely.

"That's what we all thought, except George hated the sea! He didn't seem to mind the river, because my father often used to take him on a trip up and down to Saltcombe in the *Sarah Jane*, but not out to sea. He was terrified of deep water."

"So why should anyone want to kill him?" asked Erwin, suddenly becoming more serious.

Jeremy gestured helplessly.

"It's a complete mystery to all of us," he replied. "Really, George was a very quiet and inoffensive little man. I can only think it was a case of mistaken identity, or else it was someone he'd upset in business, maybe."

"But that would mean they must have known he was staying here at West Winds," pointed out Erwin logically. "And besides, it seems that it was your father's gun that was used to kill him."

"Well, I simply don't understand it. First Rachel and now George. It makes me wonder if anyone else is going to be next."

"A very reasonable assumption," agreed Erwin, "especially if you're a devotee of fictional whodunits." He allowed himself a few moments' pause. "Tell me, Mr

Seabourne, why did you take George's car up to London so soon after you heard about Rachel's murder? If that had been me, I think I would have been too shocked and upset even to think of carrying on with business as usual."

"Because it had already been arranged," explained Jeremy. "And however insensitive it might have looked, life has to go on. George came down in a Porsche last Friday and asked me as soon as he arrived if I could take it back on Monday because he was staying for a few days, and it was needed for a customer. He'd brought it down for a test drive – it was something he often did. When you run a garage selling expensive cars, you often take whatever chance you can to try them out."

"So if George was left here without a car," said Erwin, "how was he intending to get back when he decided it was time to leave?"

Jeremy smiled.

"That's simple," he answered. "I returned last night in his Aston Martin, and he would have gone back to London in that. The advantage of working in the car trade is you can use whatever vehicle you like. We only sell top of the range cars, so it always makes for a pleasurable journey to and fro."

"You're obviously a man who enjoys his job," conceded Erwin light-heartedly, and then changed his tone suddenly. "Did you know that the *Sarah Jane* has gone?"

Jeremy looked blankly at him.

"Gone? What do you mean?"

"Gone, as in it's no longer at its mooring. It disappeared in the middle of last night, at about the time you were arriving back from London, possibly."

"Well of course I didn't know! Has it been stolen?"

"Taking all the circumstances into careful consideration, Mr Seabourne, it made me wonder if your father had anything to do with it."

"But that would mean – it would mean – no, it couldn't have been Dad! That's impossible!"

"I'm inclined to agree with you," said Erwin. "Although it *looks* very much as though your father is involved in it, I don't think he's got anything to do with it at all."

22

Back To Saltcombe

Erwin and I had returned to his car and were sitting inside, silently staring at the river. The rest of our conversation with Jeremy had yielded little new information, other than the fact that George Bland's body had been removed from the house and a team of police investigators were continuing the painstaking search of the house and grounds for forensic evidence. Minkie Seabourne and Catherine were both deeply shocked by what had happened but seemed to be coping with it and Rosanna Brown was looking after them. Superintendent Haworth was trying to establish the whereabouts of Charles Seabourne by every means available, but all business connections had so far drawn a blank. It was disconcerting to think that an armed assailant might still be prowling around.

Erwin's expression was at its most enigmatic. He had spent the last few minutes trying to work out how to find the *Sarah Jane*, but the task seemed impossible. Even a cabin cruiser with a distinctly old-fashioned appearance would be difficult to find amongst the many boats and watercraft that were tied up along the estuary and in the sea around Saltcombe. And there was always the possibility, of course, that it was hidden away somewhere. At last he came to a decision.

"The answer *must* be in Saltcombe," he said. "Whoever took the *Sarah Jane*, they're not going to risk sailing it out to sea. I think we're going to find it there, and I have an idea where it *might* be."

He reached for the car's ignition switch and started the engine. Soon we were driving along the road that led past Smallbury to the seaside resort. It was turning out to be a rather grey overcast morning and the sky looked as though it might begin to rain. By the time we entered Saltcombe twenty minutes later, a light drizzle was starting to fall. Even the most attractive town can be made to appear miserably uninviting, and people were trudging around in coats, holding up umbrellas. It was a dismal spectacle. Out on the water, there were dozens of yachts and motor boats of all shapes and sizes, much as I had seen on our river cruise the previous Saturday evening. Was the *Sarah Jane* lying out there amongst them? If so, it would certainly be very difficult to spot.

But Erwin had other plans. He found a place near the harbour to park the car and we got out.

"There's the lifeboat station," he commented, pointing to a building at the end of the harbour with the distinctive look of a large boathouse from which a long slipway ran down into the water. "They had a new lifeboat last year, replacing the old one which had been in service for over thirty years. The crew are all local volunteers, like young Mr Fairweather. See the other boats in the harbour? They're mostly trawlers and crabbers, and that's the pier over there where the Torbay ferry comes in. And at the far end," he went on, drawing my attention to a collection of buildings beneath the steep wooden hillside that rose high above the harbour, "you can see Wallace's Boatyard, where Robert Fairweather works. He's very conveniently situated for when the lifeboat gets called out, isn't he?"

I was only half-listening to what Erwin was saying because my attention kept wandering back to the grey choppy sea and the dozens of boats dotted around, each moored to its float. Disregarding the yachts with their tall masts, I searched with my eyes among the small boats and cabin cruisers for anything that looked like the familiar lines of the *Sarah Jane*, but no matter how hard I stared out into the misty murkiness I could see nothing that resembled Charles Seabourne's old wooden-hulled boat.

Erwin smiled at me and shook his head.

"I don't think you're going to find it out there in the open water," he remarked. "That would be too much to expect. I think we shall need to look a little more carefully and selectively. Let's take a stroll."

Although he made it sound casual, I think he already had a good idea of where to look but did not wish to reveal it too soon, like a conjurer about to perform a difficult trick, as if he were trying to keep me in suspense. I felt certain he had spent far too much of his time reading detective novels and had now decided to start behaving like one of his favourite characters, for fictional sleuths always seem to have an annoying habit of keeping important clues to themselves. We followed the road, which was not much more than a rutted lane, that led away from the harbour and passed behind Wallace's Boatyard until eventually it stopped altogether at the next headland, beyond which there was only a rough footpath following the rocky terrain beside the water's edge. The cliff rose steeply beside us, with a woodland of ancient trees overhanging far above our heads. We stumbled along the path for quite a distance, picking our way carefully over the uneven ground, and then we reached a small promontory where the path turned sharply around a corner, and there we found a rather quaint and dilapidated old boathouse standing alone in a tiny secluded bay. It was one of those buildings that you never expect to come across, even though you know they exist. It was built on a ledge of rock and jutted out into the water, but from where we were standing we could see the entire structure: a narrow two-storey building constructed of local stone, with a pitched roof of slates, two big wooden doors at river level covering the boat entrance, and above that, a balcony with a door and two windows set in the stonework of the gable-end wall, giving an unrestricted view out over the river. There was a door in the side wall which provided access to the lower part of the building, and the main entrance leading directly to the upper floor was another door around the back, where the path needed to ascend to higher ground in order to gain access to it.

The condition of the building was poor, and there seemed to be a general air of neglect, as if nobody could be bothered with it any more. It belonged to one of the big houses at the top of the cliff, and was reached by a flight of stone steps cut into the craggy towering rock. The steps ended at a small wicket gate marked "Private" with the name of the property indicated beneath it on a wooden nameplate, although it was too far away for me to be able to read it.

"What a secluded place," I said, marvelling at the sight of leafy riverside trees spreading their branches over the rooftop, almost hiding it from view. It had an unquestionable appearance of loss and decay about it, suggesting that it had seen better days, a sad and lonely remnant from a previous age of great affluence that had now vanished leaving a bare and deserted reminder of the past, with its broken and rotting wooden doors, dirty cobweb-infested windows and rusting locks and hinges. Nobody cared for it any longer, it stood like an unwanted outcast, its glorious halcyon days gone forever, leaving nothing more than a forlorn abandoned fragment of a lost era. The pleasure boats of the rich these days were kept on show for all to see, their gleaming hulls resplendent in the open waterways, not hidden away from the world like prized possessions.

"I shouldn't think anybody ever comes down here, it's completely undisturbed," said Erwin.

"However did you know it existed?" I asked.

"Because it belongs to Seaview House and James Carvell told me about it – he referred to the old family boathouse which his father would have used at one time when he had his own boat. I looked it up on an old map and there it was. Seaview House might be a hotel today, but in the past it would have been a large private residence for one of Saltcombe's wealthier inhabitants. Besides, James's father was a member of the Royal Saltcombe Golf Club so he must have been quite well to do himself. Let's go and take a closer look at it."

We walked on and approached the building from river level, and as the tide was still well out we were able to reach it across the small bay, although the water came up past the bottom of the two big doors. On closer inspection, they consisted of long vertical wooden slats with spaces in between, mounted on sturdy frames, so that they could each be opened and closed even in the deepest water of a spring tide when the river water would flow easily through the gaps in the wood with little resistance.

Erwin did not seem too inclined to wade into the water in order to look through these gaps. Instead, he walked up the side of the building to the door set in the wall at the rear end. From a distance I would have said that the hinges were rusted solid and I should have seriously doubted whether the ancient door had been opened for many years, but as we drew nearer I noticed in surprise that the hinges had been treated with some liquid substance and the lock looked new.

Erwin examined the door carefully, ran his finger down one hinge and showed me a trace of fresh oil.

"This has been done recently," he murmured quietly. "Someone has been here in the last few days."

He tested the padlock but it held securely. Although the door looked shabby, the timber was in sound condition and there was not the slightest trace of rot present, so there were no gaps or cracks for us to peer through. Erwin stood back to take a better look at the building. There were two small windows along the side, covered in layers of grime. Some of it was on the inside, but there was dirt and muck on the outside too, and Erwin took a handkerchief out of his pocket, went down to the water's edge, moistened it in the river and returned to wipe it carefully against one pane of glass. Gradually the dirt came away, leaving not a clean window but one that was less opaque. He put his face up close to the glass in order to look inside the boathouse and it took him a few seconds to make out the shape of something within the building.

"Ah!" he breathed, and I could see from his expression that his eyes were shining with a brightness I had never seen before. He stepped aside. "Take a look. I thought it might be here, and I was right!"

I went up to the window and strained my eyes to see inside. Everything was dark, but I could make out the shape of something large within the building – something that seemed to fill the otherwise bare interior – and then I almost recoiled with shock when I realised that I was looking at the outline of the *Sarah Jane*.

"But why *here*?" I asked in little more than a stunned whisper.

"Someone wanted to get it out of the way, and succeeded," said Erwin thoughtfully. "The question is, *why* did they want to get it out of the way.....but now we've found it, I know the answer."

I pointed to the small wicket gate nearby where the wooden nameplate distinctly bore the name Seaview House, confirming what Erwin had said.

"If this place belongs to the Carvells, it must be James," I stated logically.

"Possibly," replied Erwin slowly, "but not necessarily. This building may *belong* to them, but it's a long way down from the house, situated in a very remote bay – look up there at those steps, they're all overgrown – so the fact that the *Sarah Jane* is tucked away inside their boathouse does not actually prove that it was James – or Julie – who put it there. They may know nothing about it at all."

I stared at him.

"But that's a bit far-fetched!" I protested.

"Oh yes, I agree – but do you see my point? There's a possibility that it's been done without their knowledge. After all, surely you might think it's more likely that Charles put it inside here to get it out of the way."

"Of course, I was forgetting about Charles."

Erwin looked at me reproachfully.

"How could you forget the man who seems to be at the very centre of the puzzle? Anyway," he went on in a rather disconcerting change of direction, "I've long since discounted Charles from being involved."

"You *don't* think he's involved?" I repeated faintly. "But he killed George Bland!"

"Did he?" said Erwin in surprise. "We have no evidence to show that he did."

"Bland was shot with his revolver!"

"That may well be the case, but it doesn't prove that Charles pulled the trigger."

"Oh, I'm getting confused!" I cried in exasperation.

"Yes," said Erwin, "I was confused in the beginning, but now I fully understand what happened. It's time I made a couple of telephone calls, and then I think we might be able to unmask the murderer in what was, I believe, a very clever plot that went ever so slightly wrong."

23

I Discover How It Was Done

Superintendent Howarth was standing beside the tidal road at the bottom of the hill from West Winds, near the two lines of wooden marker posts, when Erwin and I drove up in the little car, and he turned to watch us approaching with an expressionless face. For once I was pleased to see him, representing as he did the force of law and order in what seemed to be an otherwise chaotic world of deceit and half-truths set against one of the most peaceful landscapes it was possible to imagine. Given the background to the mystery, that I was originally his main suspect and Erwin some will-o-the-wisp itinerant artist, it might have been considered possible that he was intent on arresting us on the spot for wasting his precious time, but it was more than evident that Erwin had succeeded in weaving a powerful spell which had the effect of causing Howarth to take him very seriously. Erwin drove past him and pulled the car off the road, parking it in the place where we had left it previously, on the footpath frequented by dog walkers.

We got out of the vehicle and joined him on the road, which was now completely dry after the last tide, with the river now at its lowest point.

"I hope you know what you're doing," he remarked laconically. "Otherwise I can see myself saying goodbye to my pension."

"Nothing as bad as that," said Erwin briskly. "If I'm wrong, which I am not, you can lock me up instead."

"You seem very sure of yourself," said Howarth.

"Superintendent," went on Erwin, "have you done everything I asked you to do?"

"Yes," said the policeman, "and that's what worries me."

"Are they all up at the house?"

"I've sent cars to collect them and everyone is there."

"All the names I gave you?"

"All the names you gave me," said Howarth. "Mrs Seabourne, her son Jeremy and daughter Catherine were already there, of course, and I have officers ensuring that they remain so."

Erwin rubbed his hands together in anticipation.

"Well by the time we have finished, you will have your murderer under arrest."

"I wish I could share your confidence."

"This is why I wanted to meet you down here, before we go up to the house," said Erwin. "I shall explain to you the background to the case, with a little topographical exposition."

Superintendent Howarth looked momentarily puzzled.

"The lie of the land is very important to understanding what happened," went on Erwin. "It all seems very complicated, but in fact it is quite straightforward, and I shall explain why."

"Please do," murmured Howarth, adopting a more relaxed posture to hear the explanation.

"From where we are standing, we can see all the important elements in the murder, with the exception of one. If we look up the hill, we can see West Winds. If we look in the opposite direction, partly hidden by trees on the high ground overlooking the river, we can see Skylark Farm where Rachel lived. Below that, where the river bends, is the place where her body was found. That one exception – the thing we cannot see – should be over there, moored on the sandbank in the middle of the river, and I'm referring to the Seabournes' cabin cruiser *Sarah Jane*, which has now disappeared. Are you with me so far?"

"Of course," replied the superintendent.

"Let us go back and consider the following: on the night of the murder, when the river is at high tide and much of the road is covered with water, Godfrey takes Rachel home to Skylark Farm from the house-party at West Winds, but because the road is impassable they drive the long way around. He drops her off just before midnight, having driven almost up to the front door of the farmhouse. He could hardly have imagined that she would come to any harm, being just a few yards from the house. But after he drives off, instead of going straight

261

into the house, Rachel makes her way over to the stable to see that all is well with her horse for the night. And it is whilst she is at the stable that something catches her eye in the distance – a light in a place where it shouldn't be. She knows that somebody is on board the *Sarah Jane*. So why not simply ignore it? After all, she and several other people, including Godfrey, had been out in it only a couple of hours earlier. Might it not be that one of the group had inadvertently left something on board and gone back to fetch it? Why should she feel compelled to go and investigate, for that is what she must have done. I doubt if we will ever know the answer to her motivation, but she went down the steep path joining her farm with the tidal road, took off her shoes and made her way over to the *Sarah Jane*, where she must have surprised whoever was on board. She saw something she was not meant to see, and had to be silenced. She received a single stab wound in the back, and if she didn't die immediately, she drowned after being dragged several hundred yards upriver and dumped in the mud. When she was attacked, she probably dropped her shoes in the river and they were carried away in the water and eventually washed out to sea. The perpetrator presumably finished whatever needed to be done on board the *Sarah Jane* and escaped. The method of effecting that escape was a puzzle at first, but once all the pieces of the mystery fell into place, it was quite straightforward – the murderer escaped on the river."

"On the river?" interrupted Howarth. "How do you

know that? Why not on foot or by car?"

"Because what drew Rachel near to the river to investigate the strange sighting was the fact that she saw *two* boats," said Erwin triumphantly. "The *Sarah Jane* had been joined by another boat."

I glanced across at the superintendent and there was now a keen expression on his face and his eyes were staring intently at Erwin.

"Go on," he breathed.

Erwin was clearly enjoying himself.

"Somebody was using the *Sarah Jane* for a clandestine purpose, and it involved the use of a second craft."

"Smuggling," said Howarth, nodding his head slowly.

"Indeed, the running ashore of something that was prohibited by law," agreed Erwin. "We can only guess at the moment what that might have been — for our purpose, it is not very important what it was. But its discovery meant that Rachel had to die."

I interrupted Erwin at this point. "Do you mean it had nothing to do with love affairs and jealousy?"

"Nothing whatsoever — I think you will find that the love affair angle played a secondary role, serving as an important diversion to hide the identity of the culprit."

"But who killed George Bland? You're forgetting that there was a second murder!"

Erwin turned to me with a faint smile. "My dear Godfrey, I am hardly likely to overlook the fact that there have also been two other murders."

"Two?"

Superintendent Howarth broke in at this point. "Mr Graham, I am investigating two murders, those of Rachel Summers and George Bland," he said patiently, but the tone of his voice suggested that he was waiting for Erwin to reveal something of which he was unaware.

"No, Superintendent, you may not realise it yet but you are actually investigating three murders. Charles Seabourne is dead, too, only his body has not been discovered."

Howarth drew a deep breath, as if Erwin had articulated something that he already suspected, and he began nodding his head slowly.

"You still seem to be several steps ahead of me," he said, "but I'm beginning to understand your line of reasoning."

Erwin bowed graciously. "Thank you," he replied. "There is no doubt in my mind that Rachel's murder set off a sequence of events which may, or may not, have been planned anyway, but what is clear to me is that a smuggling operation had been established, probably for quite some period of time, and it was operating successfully without drawing attention to itself. Apart from those directly involved in it, nobody else was aware of what was going on because it was brilliantly conceived and well carried out. And now," he said, "I think it is time we made our way up to the house and confronted everyone with the truth. Shall we drive up there or walk?"

Superintendent Howarth cast a dubious look at the old car. "I think I'll walk," he said.

"In that case we'll walk up with you. But first of all I must fetch something." Erwin hurried over to the vehicle and took a bag out from behind the driver's seat. Howarth looked at the bag with a puzzled frown but had the sense not to ask what was in it, for Erwin would undoubtedly have prevaricated. He was behaving like a small boy who does not wish to give away his secrets.

We walked in silence along the tidal road and followed it up the hill until we reached the gates of West Winds, where a uniformed police constable was standing. Howarth nodded to him and he stood to attention. We made our way up the drive and another policeman in uniform was positioned by the front door. He stepped across quickly to open the door for his superior, and Howarth acknowledged his action with a grunt of thanks.

Rosanna Brown was standing in the middle of the hall, waiting for us.

"Everyone is in the lounge," she informed us solemnly, looking mostly at the superintendent. Then I saw her catch Erwin's eye and give him a slight nod of the head. I wondered what was going on, it all seemed rather unreal. She turned and walked ahead of us, opening the lounge doors for us to enter the room. Superintendent Howarth led the way, followed closely by Erwin and then myself.

The scene inside the lounge resembled a tableau, everyone within the room either seated or standing, and completely motionless. Rosanna quietly closed the doors behind us, and then I noticed Sergeant Hoskins standing over by the French windows. Minkie Seabourne was sitting on the chaise longue in her usual upright posture, legs elegantly crossed, looking straight ahead at the far wall of the room as though deep in thought; Jeremy was standing by the fireplace, in much the same position as when I first saw him on the evening of the house-party, but this time Emma was closely at his side; Catherine was seated in an armchair, trying to appear composed, although her face bore an intensely worried expression; James and Julie Carvell were sitting side by side on the settee, holding hands but looking distantly in opposite directions; and Robert Fairweather was standing on his own, near to Sergeant Hoskins. Our entrance caused them all, one by one, to shift their gaze in our direction.

"All present and correct, Sergeant Hoskins?" asked Superintendent Howarth vigorously.

"Yes, sir, everyone you requested to be here is in the room," replied Hoskins with the self-satisfied look of a subordinate who has done his job efficiently by getting them all there, even though it probably hadn't been an easy task.

Howarth looked around at each of their faces, now turned to watch him with varying degrees of interest.

"Good," he said. "I expect you all know why you've been asked to come here today."

"As a matter of fact," replied James Carvell, "the reason was not made terribly clear, and it is quite inconvenient for both my wife and myself to be away from our business – we're hoping this will not take too long."

"It will take as long as necessary," said Howarth curtly.

"Serious crimes have been committed and each one of you is under suspicion."

James Carvell opened his mouth to say something, but then he thought better of it and remained silent whilst his wife gave him a sharp nudge. I noticed that Robert Fairweather was looking intently in my direction, wondering perhaps if I was also one of the suspects. That would hardly have been surprising, since everyone had assumed from the outset that I had murdered Rachel.

"Now," continued Superintendent Howarth, "I know you have all met Mr Graham, who is an investigative journalist. Mr Graham has come up with a theory, and he has asked me if he can come along today in order to put that theory to the test. He may also want to ask you one or two questions."

"This is ridiculous," said James suddenly, jumping to his feet. "You, a policeman, is asking this reporter to test some theory? Theory about what? Surely this is a police investigation, not some sensational inquiry conducted by the press? And what is *he* doing here?" James pointed at me. "That's the man Rachel brought to this house on the night of her death!" I could see the accusing look in his eyes.

Erwin stepped forward. "Let me make one thing absolutely clear to everyone in this room," he said in a quiet but authoritative voice, "Godfrey Sanderson did not kill Rachel Summers. He knew her in the few days before her death, but that is all. By circumstance only, he immediately fell under suspicion, and yet circumstantial evidence could well have led to him being charged with Rachel's murder, but that would only have let her real killer go free. We are here today because I have been able to unravel the mystery – my theory, as the superintendent puts it – and in a few minutes everyone will know who killed Rachel Summers and why." There was a sudden outburst of exclamations, and Erwin held his hand up for silence. "And when you know who killed Rachel Summers, you will also know who killed George Bland" he gave an imperceptible pause "and Charles Seabourne."

There was a loud cry of anguish from Minkie Seabourne. "What do you mean about Charles?"

"I mean, Mrs Seabourne," said Erwin, "that your husband is dead as well."

Jeremy Seabourne stepped forward from the fireplace and his mouth was open but no words came out. He sat down suddenly in a nearby chair. Catherine Seabourne had gone white in the face and stared helplessly from one to the other of us. At last she managed to speak.

"But he can't be dead," she said in a hushed voice, "he's gone away on a business trip."

"Really?" said Erwin. "Can you tell me where he's gone?"

"Well no, but he has regular business dealings all over the country."

"How did he go?"

"He took the car, of course."

"His own car?"

"Yes!"

"And would you mind telling me what car your father drives?"

"It's a Bentley."

"A white one?"

"Yes."

"When he's at home, where does he keep his white Bentley?"

"It's always standing outside the front of the house, at the top of the drive, where we park all our cars."

"But you do have a large garage behind the house?"

"Well yes, but he rarely uses it!" said Catherine in exasperation.

"So would it come as a surprise to you if you were to find his Bentley parked in the garage at this very moment?" asked Erwin. The room broke out into a buzz of frenzied conversation.

Superintendent Howarth took control of the situation with a raised voice. "Sergeant Hoskins, will you please accompany Miss Seabourne out to the garage in order to ascertain whether her father's car is parked inside it or not."

The room fell silent again while the sergeant led Catherine out of the lounge and they were gone for several minutes. When they came back, Catherine was crying.

"I don't understand it," she said in a distraught voice.

"Is your father's Bentley in the garage?" asked Erwin.

"Yes!"

"Was there anything unusual about it?"

"It was covered over by a dust-sheet."

"The sort that you put over a car when it's stored for a period of time?"

"Yes. My father sometimes covers it in the winter."

I glanced quickly over at Minkie Seabourne, but her face had no emotion on it whatsoever, she seemed to have shut herself off from her surroundings.

"How did you know it was there?" asked Catherine in a whisper.

"Based on my deductions, I guessed that it was there," said Erwin, "so I rang earlier and spoke to your housekeeper, Mrs Brown, and asked her to check for me. I know the garage is in a secluded place behind trees and hedges and cannot be seen easily from the house, and I also know that you have to unlock the garage door in order to see inside. Mrs Brown went to have a look and came back on the telephone to say that the Bentley was parked inside, under a cover. You see, Miss Seabourne, I had a very strong suspicion that your father had not gone away on this supposed business trip that everyone kept referring to."

"So if he never left the house, it was Charles who shot George Bland!" exclaimed Robert Fairweather dramatically.

"That would certainly seem to be the most likely explanation," agreed Erwin, "especially as George Bland was shot with Charles's revolver. The only problem is, I believe that Charles Seabourne was already dead when George Bland was murdered, so that makes it very

270

difficult for him to have committed the crime." There was a general look of disbelief and puzzlement in the room, as if the assembled gathering could not comprehend what he was saying. "Superintendent Howarth," went on Erwin, "I think it's time to reveal what I believe really happened."

Howarth made a deprecating gesture, and Erwin suddenly had everyone's full attention. The only sound in the room, apart from his quiet voice, was the clock ticking on the mantelpiece.

"And so," continued Erwin with a wry smile, "we reach that point, in the grand old tradition of the country house murder, where the culprit is unmasked in the denouement. It has all the right ingredients of a classic whodunit – sex, jealousy, avarice, and it all begins with that seemingly most innocuous of things, a rickety old cabin cruiser, the *Sarah Jane,* which Charles Seabourne purchased in Henley-on-Thames one day many years ago and sailed it down the English Channel in an epic voyage worthy of a Hammond Innes novel. It was one of those wooden-hulled vessels of the 1940s and 1950s, so much admired by our friend here, Mr Fairweather. Indeed, it went to Wallace's Boatyard in Saltcombe to be repaired and put back into seaworthy condition, enabling it to do cross-channel trips to France, from where you may be quite sure it brought back with it many a case of fine wines. And perhaps it was this that gave somebody an idea that if it could bring back bottles from the best French vineyards, so it could bring back other things, too.

Items, let us say, that could not lawfully be imported into this country. The *Sarah Jane* was about to embark on a new career of smuggling. There was, however, one slight problem. It's all very well for the *Sarah Jane* to make legitimate family crossings of the English Channel, but what if somebody was intending to do crossings in secret? Sooner or later, the boat's absence from its river mooring would be noticed. And so a very clever plan was put into action, one that I suspect only two people knew about. The *Sarah Jane* would be used to run to and fro across the channel, probably at night, but it was important that she should never leave her mooring! The answer to the problem was to have *two Sarah Janes!* Two identical cabin cruisers that could be swapped back and fore, without anyone noticing."

"Two *Sarah Janes?*" repeated Jeremy incredulously. "Are you out of your mind? You don't know what you're talking about! Do you seriously expect us to believe that there could be two versions of the same boat and nobody noticed?"

"But that's where you're wrong," said Erwin gently with a smile, "it *was* noticed. I have carefully taken note of things that were said. It seems that on the night of the house-party, Rachel remarked that a handrail appeared to be in a different place, even though it was impossible to explain why. Then, when I called to see the Carvells in their guest house and spoke to James, he referred to having stayed on board and noticed that the bunk had seemed less comfortable on one occasion than on

272

another. What is your opinion, Mr Fairweather? Is it possible or am I talking nonsense?"

Robert Fairweather stepped forward into the middle of the room. "It's quite possible," he replied, "though frankly I think it rather unlikely. Obviously cabin cruisers like *Sarah Jane,* being wooden-hulled vessels, were individually hand-built to a pattern so you would expect to find certain types looking alike, but on the same stretch of river? You say that Rachel thought the handrail was in a different place and James commented on the comfort of the bunk, but neither of those seem to me to be anything more than fleeting impressions, they are hardly evidence of there being two boats." He shrugged. "But you may be right, I don't know."

"Let us, for the moment, assume that I *am* right," said Erwin with a degree of smugness that suggested he could hardly be anything else – I was quickly coming to recognise this characteristic of his which, in other people of lesser personality, would be considered quite sickening. "There *were* two cabin cruisers, sufficiently alike to fool everybody. One was kept at its usual mooring on the river below West Winds, the other was hidden away from view elsewhere, and from time to time they were swapped around, as and when required for the purpose of smuggling. Now let us consider where that hideaway might be. Mr Carvell, can you think of anywhere?"

James Carvell looked startled. "*Me?* Why should I have any idea?"

"Oh, come now, don't seem so surprised. Do you not

273

own a boathouse?"

"Well yes, of course I do. But it's been empty for years – it's where my father used to keep his boat until he got rid of it."

"Let me ask you an important question, Mr Carvell, and think carefully before you answer," said Erwin. "I am aware that the boathouse is a long way down the cliff from your guest house, connected to it by a steep flight of steps cut into the rockface, but you seem quite a fit young man. When did you last go down to pay it a visit?"

"*I* don't know! Ages ago! I've got no reason to go down to it. It's just an old disused building on our land!"

"It might well be on your land, Mr Carvell, but it's certainly not disused. This morning, at approximately half-past ten, there was a boat sitting inside it and that boat was none other than the *Sarah Jane*."

There was a loud gasp of surprise from the assembled group.

James Carvell's lip was quivering. "But that's impossible!"

Erwin turned to the large policeman standing by his side. "Superintendent Howarth, would you care to comment?"

"At some time before eleven o' clock this morning," began Howarth in his ponderous voice, "I received a telephone call from Mr Graham, explaining that he was in Saltcombe. He said he had made a discovery of great importance to the case, and when I asked him what it was, he told me that the *Sarah Jane*, which had disappeared from its mooring on the river, was hidden inside the boathouse belonging to Seaview House. I sent two of my officers to verify this information, without drawing attention to themselves, and they later reported back to me that it was correct."

James Carvell had gone white in the face and his eyes were staring with an almost blank expression. He did not say anything.

"But that still only accounts for one *Sarah Jane,*" continued Erwin. "So where is the other one, whether it be the original or the copy? If my reasoning is correct, it is lying at the bottom of the sea in the English Channel some distance out from Saltcombe, and inside its cabin is the body of Charles Seabourne!"

"No!" cried out Minkie Seabourne. "No, I refuse to believe it!"

Jeremy and Catherine were both shaking their heads in disbelief.

"It can't be true!" said Jeremy in a hushed voice after a few moments. "Can it?"

"I'm afraid it is very much the truth," said Erwin, "and there is one person in this room who knows only too well that it is the truth. Is that not so, Mr Fairweather?"

Now it was Robert Fairweather's turn to stare, and he began to laugh nervously.

"How should I know?" he replied in a faltering stammer.

"Because you stabbed Rachel Summers to death when she discovered what you were up to, and then you cleverly arranged to use an impending business trip that Charles Seabourne was due to undertake in order to murder him and dispose of his body in such a way that his disappearance would cast suspicion on him, and finally you shot your business partner George Bland because he was the only one who could work out that you were Rachel's killer. You knew that your action in murdering him would be blamed on the elusive Charles Seabourne, whose revolver had mysteriously vanished with the man himself."

"But this is quite preposterous!" laughed Robert Fairweather, looking around the room. "It's got nothing to do with me at all!"

"Since you are so reluctant to accept the blame," said Erwin Graham in a calm voice, "let me explain to everyone the events that led up to this series of appalling murders. Watersford is one of those delightfully quiet Devonshire villages where nothing ever happens. If you look in the parish records, you will probably find that nothing has *ever* happened, apart from a bit of sheep stealing now and again. But because it has a lovely picturesque river near the coast, with Saltcombe only a few miles downstream, it starts to attract people who have made money and want to live amidst this wonderful scenery. They build mansions for themselves, and so affluent members of society come to live here, and it is easy enough to get back and fore to London, where many of them have their businesses. One such family is the Seabournes, but they have lived here so long they now consider themselves to be true Devonians – indeed, I imagine that Jeremy and Catherine were born here. And Charles's business partner, George Bland, is almost adopted, too, he spends so much of his time here – why, he even thinks of buying a hotel in Saltcombe. But George Bland, the quiet, unassuming friend and associate of Charles, is the key to what has happened, because he sees a new opportunity to add to his list of business successes. Not content with the profits from his legitimate concerns, such as the car dealership that Jeremy works for – Jeremy, the feckless son of the household who doesn't really want to work too hard for his living, and therefore becomes a wonderful pawn in George's new venture – no, Mr Bland decides to use the Seabournes to further his ambitions with a smuggling racket. Are you all with me so far?"

Superintendent Howarth nodded grimly. "Go on," he said.

"And that, I believe, is the essence of it: the Seabournes were unaware that they were being *used* by the man they considered to be their friend – and maybe it went a bit deeper than friendship." Erwin cast a glance towards Minkie Seabourne, who retained her cool, elegant poise. "Anyway, at some point George Bland decided that the *Sarah Jane's* frequent pleasure crossings to France was an opportunity too good to miss, and he could use the cabin cruiser to bring goods into the country. But George was not a particular keen sailor and did not relish making the crossings himself, he needed an assistant who had access

277

to the boat – but even that presented one or two problems. George Bland formed a friendship with one of the family's regular visitors, Robert Fairweather, and Mr Fairweather was the perfect partner. Not only was he an experienced sailor, serving on the Saltcombe lifeboat crew, but also he worked for a boat-building company – the very same one that restored the *Sarah Jane!* And he was obsessed with wooden boats! One or other of them, probably Robert, came up with the idea of the two identical *Sarah Janes*, and from then on it was a simple matter of using the one whilst the other was safely tied up in the river below West Winds. George Bland's visits always seemed to coincide with high water at midnight, and now we know why. He would always be around to receive the goods, which Jeremy would unwittingly take back to London in whatever car he was using, a car from George Bland's showroom. Of course, there was the slight problem of hiding the second *Sarah Jane* somewhere out of sight so that there was never any risk of the two being seen in daylight, and James Carvell, without realising it, provided his boathouse at the bottom of the cliff. No wonder George kept asking if he would sell Seaview House to him! He would have had the ownership of the boathouse himself then!"

"A very clever plan," said Howarth slowly, nodding his understanding of it.

"And it could have gone on for a very long time," conceded Erwin, "but it was stopped in its tracks on the night of the last house-party, when everything was set to run as usual. It didn't even matter that the *Sarah Jane* was used for a jaunt down to Saltcombe – Robert Fairweather had the second boat, loaded up with whatever they were bringing into the country, hidden away in the Carvells' boathouse, and all he had to do was slip away early from the party, fetch the second *Sarah Jane* and sail it upriver to switch them over in complete darkness. Unfortunately, he did not reckon with Rachel seeing to her horse last thing when she arrived home just before midnight, or that she would notice strange lights on the river and go down to investigate. Rachel, poor thing, sees the two boats and probably calls out to Robert to ask what's going on. And Robert Fairweather knows immediately that he cannot allow Rachel to tell anyone what she has seen. Perhaps he engages her in harmless conversation to gain her confidence, and then" Erwin suddenly reached into the bag he was carrying and pulled out the marlinspike that he had retrieved from the *Sarah Jane* "he stabbed her viciously with this!"

Another loud gasp went around the room.

Erwin fixed his eyes on Robert Fairweather. "Although it has been cleaned, I have examined it carefully and there are minute traces of blood on it, together with what appears to be a fingerprint. It did not take you long to drag Rachel's body some distance along the river, dump her face down in the mud and return to the two boats, where you completed the switch and took the first *Sarah Jane* back to the boathouse. But you knew you had a problem: Rachel's body would be found and this would

279

lead to a murder investigation. Godfrey, of course, would be the obvious suspect, but this was not good enough for you. Knowing the family well, you also knew about Rachel's broken-off engagement to Jeremy, and her affair with Charles, which had led to her becoming pregnant. Thinking quickly, it seemed to you that Charles might be considered a possible suspect if Godfrey could somehow prove his innocence, and you knew that Charles was about to go away on a business trip. You thought up some pretext to get him on his own, and lured him into the second *Sarah Jane*, which was now at the mooring. I would hazard a guess that you had already stolen his revolver from the house, so you shot him dead on the boat and then sailed it out to sea, where you scuttled it, making your escape in the dinghy. A hazardous undertaking, but you were a desperate man. Back on land, you made your way to the Carvells' boathouse, got the first *Sarah Jane* out and took it back to its mooring on the river below here. The goods had already been brought ashore by you and George Bland and put in the boot of the car that Jeremy was taking back to London. You also had to hide Charles's Bentley, having probably retrieved the keys from his pocket after he was dead, so you came back in the middle of the night and hid it in the garage, putting the dust-cover over it in a way that he would have done himself. That left just one loose end for you to clear up. You knew that George Bland must have suspected that you were Rachel's murderer – after all, he knew exactly what was going on down on the river. So you used Charles's revolver to murder Bland, knowing that Charles – who had mysteriously vanished – would be the chief suspect. But Charles, as we now know, was already lying dead on the sea-bed in the cabin of the sunken second *Sarah Jane*."

Erwin stopped speaking and there was complete silence in the room. His breathtaking performance had left everyone stunned, myself included. Superintendent Howarth stepped forward and said, "Robert Fairweather, I am arresting you on suspicion of the murder of..." but he got no further than that, for the young man had reached his hand quickly into his pocket and pulled out Charles's revolver, which he pointed straight at the policeman.

"Come one step nearer to me and I will shoot you," said Robert Fairweather, and started walking towards the French windows. "You, too," he said to Sergeant Hoskins, "get back or you're a dead man."

And then an extraordinary thing happened, one of those events that not even a writer of fiction could dream up. Before Fairweather reached the doors that led out onto the terrace, one of them opened and a gipsy woman came into the room, so outlandish a figure that she brought the proceedings to an abrupt halt.

"*You!*" gasped Robert Fairweather, staring straight at her.

"Yes," said Belle, "me. And you might as well stop pointing that gun at me because it's not loaded."

Like a scene from a film, he looked stupidly at the

revolver in his hand and pulled the trigger, expecting it to go off bang, but nothing happened except for a metallic click. Furiously, he pulled the trigger again and again, but it made the same harmless noise. Hoskins saw his chance and leapt forward, bringing Robert Fairweather crashing to the floor.

"Oh," said Belle with a beaming smile, "did I come in at the right moment?"

24

In Conclusion

"I don't normally drink on duty," said Superintendent Howarth, holding a pint of beer in his hand, "but this has to be the exception."

We were standing in a small group at the bar of The Skipper's Inn, the superintendent leaning against the counter whilst Sergeant Hoskins stood beside him, with Erwin, Belle, Rosanna Brown and myself making up the remainder. We were all relaxing with a drink.

"Of course," went on Howarth, looking directly at me, "I was all for arresting you two days ago, and I still don't know how Mr Graham here convinced me otherwise. You're a very lucky man, Mr Sanderson."

"Luck does not even *begin* to come into it," retorted Erwin pompously. "The trouble with you policemen is you jump to hasty conclusions, and once you've decided that you have the answer, you never like to admit that you might be wrong."

Howarth smiled benevolently at Erwin. "I freely admit that I jumped to a hasty conclusion, and that I was wrong."

Erwin blinked in surprise.

"How many beers have you had?" he demanded suspiciously.

"Given the circumstances, it seemed an open and shut case, as they so often are," continued the superintendent, "but you believed in Mr Sanderson's innocence and conducted a wonderful investigation of your own – not that I approve, mind you! It's the job of the police to investigate any crime that's committed."

"Huh!" snorted Belle indignantly, "and where would we be now if you'd had your way?"

"Our investigation was progressing very well," said Howarth imperiously. "My men had also found Charles Seabourne's Bentley in the garage during the course of a thorough search of the house and the grounds."

"And it probably strengthened your view that Charles was still in the locality and was George Bland's killer, as you were meant to think!" said Erwin. "In other words, you were completely misled! Now the thing is," he continued, "I knew at the outset that Godfrey was innocent, or why else would he have come to me? He is obviously not a devious man. So unless Rachel had been killed in some chance encounter with a complete stranger – which was always a remote possibility – it had to be one of her friends. That narrowed the suspects down considerably. By talking to them in turn, I was able to build up a picture of what went on between them all, and Rosanna provided invaluable background information which none of them would have told me. To begin with, this indicated that Charles was Rachel's murderer, out of jealousy, and for a while I was certain of it, particularly as he had vanished."

"So I was not the only one to be completely misled," said Superintendent Howarth, with a distinct tone of irony to his voice.

Erwin blithely ignored the interruption. "George Bland's murder only seemed to confirm it all the more. I knew that Charles's Bentley had gone, which would have been entirely in keeping with the theory of the business trip, but then I later learned that it was put in the garage to keep it out of sight, and covered with a dust-sheet as he was in the habit of doing, suggesting that he was in hiding nearby. Rosanna had drawn my attention to there being a difference in Charles's usual routine, so I felt that he had clearly not set off on business as was asserted by the family. I surmised that George Bland was having an affair with Minkie Seabourne – she and Charles were leading substantially separate lives – and this would seem to give a very clear motive for Charles murdering George, for whilst he did not mind having affairs of his own, he did not want his wife to do so. In the same way that the superintendent was convinced of Godfrey's guilt, for a while I was equally convinced it was Charles. But the *Sarah Jane* gave me cause for concern, because I felt that something was not quite right with it. Enter the smuggling theory, and suddenly everything began to look different. The idea of two identical boats, a notion almost too fanciful for words, brought the solution within my grasp. And so I sent Belle on a second errand, like the other night, in full gipsy attire, but this time I asked her to call on Robert Fairweather – he lives in a small terraced fisherman's cottage in lower Saltcombe. She talked her way into his living room, plying her lucky charms, and I gambled on the fact that if he were guilty, he might succumb to the idea of buying one of her charms, to ward off bad luck. When he left the room to find some loose change, Belle quickly searched his jacket pockets and found the revolver, which she unloaded before he came back into the room."

"There wasn't much time," said Belle, "but us gipsies are not country folk for nothing. I knew how to load and unload guns before I was five years old."

"How did you know he would have to leave the room to find loose change?" I asked. "He might have had some in his pocket."

Belle turned to me with a knowing look.

"I had him in a hypnotic spell," she said, "and I'd have sent him out of the room for something else, if necessary."

"Well, it has all worked out very satisfactorily," said Howarth, "what say you, Sergeant?"

Hoskins nodded vigorously in agreement.

"Most satisfactory indeed, I would say, sir," he replied. "I always think it's nice to get a little bit of help from the public. Makes our life so much easier."

Rosanna Brown turned to me.

"What are you going to do now?" she asked curiously, "having lived under a cloud of suspicion almost since you've been here. Will you stay in Watersford?"

"Hill Cottage is mine for the rest of the year," I said. "In the short time I have been here, I've seen tragedy and I've seen salvation. Erwin and Belle are now my dear friends, and I have them to thank for solving the tidal road mystery. It may be the first, but I'm sure it won't be the last."

Superintendent Howarth lowered his glass.

"Do you mind if I don't drink to that?" he said with a mischievous twinkle in his eye, and we all laughed.